The Whipman
is Watching

The Whipman
is Watching

T. A. Dyer

Houghton Mifflin Company   Boston   1979

Library of Congress Cataloging in Publication Data

Dyer, Thomas A
    The whipman is watching.

    SUMMARY: Thirteen-year-old Angie and her
slightly older cousin Cultus must learn to face the
problems brought on by their growing frustrations
as they find themselves caught between the world
of the Indian reservation and the white world
outside.
    [1.   Indians of North America – Fiction.
2.   Prejudices – Fiction]   I.   Title.
PZ7.D9885Wh   [Fic]   79-16631
ISBN 0-395-28581-X

2087236

To True and Eleanor Dyer

The Whipman is Watching

1

~~~~~~

Angie could hear the bus long before she could see it. That was sometimes useful. If they were late it gave the children time to run to the road. And once, hearing the bus begin its weary climb up the hill, Angie had the nerve to hide from it. Cultus, Marta, and Carysa all walked past where she hid behind a juniper tree. They saw her, but walked on by, looking straight ahead in conspiracy. When the bus stopped, her heart beat so fast that it wasn't fun anymore. Still she hid. Above her in the tree a magpie scolded, in the way Katla always said meant you were going to have bad luck. She thought the bird would give her away.

When the bus started up the hill again, she crept around the little tree the way a squirrel circles away from a dog. That part had been exciting. But Angie admitted to herself that the rest of the day had been a bore, and a hungry one, too, with no lunch.

Most of the time, however, hearing the bus was just depressing. The children usually talked, or teased, or threw rocks until they heard it. Then they stopped. And although no one ever told them to do it, they would get in a scraggly line and wait for the bus to pull up.

It was the same this morning. They heard the bus and lined up to get on it. Angie was first, as usual, so when she climbed up the steps the driver spoke to her.

"*Niih maitski,*" he said to her in Indian, "good morning." Johnson was a white man, but he knew some phrases in Angie's language. Angie walked on past him, eyes down in front of her, silent. So did the others.

It wasn't entirely because he was a white man that no one answered him. That was a big part of it, sure. But it was more because he was the bus driver. The boys just naturally tried to drive him crazy, and Cultus was the worst of the boys. Angie didn't dare speak to the driver if she wanted to avoid trouble with Cultus.

She walked down the aisle, eyes down, and sat in her seat. Above her, over the window where the curve of the roof started, the driver had scrawled their names in purple marker. "Angie-Lois," it said. Angie wondered if having a seat assigned to her should have made her angry. It didn't. She didn't have to choose where to sit, and that was about the only easy, comfortable thing about the long ride to school. And it would be easier when Lois got on.

2

Angie snuggled down next to the window. That was her place, too. Lois was her best friend, but they were different in a lot of ways. Angie liked to look out the window. She had seen the scenery a thousand times, but she always sat next to the window. And Lois never minded. Lois was more, well, social than Angie.

Angie slouched, snuggled, wedged her knees up on the back of the seat in front of her. She knew it would make her jeans silver at the knees with aluminum stains. But she could almost hide. Her legs were long enough now, at thirteen, that she could slouch with her knees wedged against the seat in front of her and still see out the window. She could almost hide from the rest of the bus this way, with just the top of her head showing.

First the bus climbed past the little valley where Katla, Angie's grandmother, would come later in the day when the morning dew was off the spring grasses and the chill out of the prairie air. Katla was gathering *humsi*, wild celery, for the Powwow. She would keep it in the refrigerator at the Longhouse until it would be served with the meals.

The bus stopped at Wehenas, at Lokees, at Smiths. The seats began to fill with familiar faces, all in their places. Angie looked without interest out the window. Juniper settlements sprouted in the sage like immigrants, stranded on their way to a better place. The rabbit brush was getting good and yellow. And the blossoms of *piakhe* and *luksh*, the roots to be harvested after *humsi*, sprinkled the prairie minutely with white.

Angie was looking out the window, but she listened tensely for signs that the usual uproar was about to begin inside the bus. She knew it wouldn't stay peaceful for long. It never did. And when the trouble began she didn't want to be part of it. It looked so quiet out on the prairie.

"Cultus is botherin' for nothin'," someone squealed. Angie didn't have to turn her head to know it was Grant Lokee. That's who Cultus sat with. The bus stopped and Mr. Johnson stood to shout something and wag his finger.

"Cultus blew his nose on me like a farmer," Grant complained with real disgust. "All over my sleeve," he added, wrestling with Cultus as he tried to rub his ·sleeve into his face. They were baiting the driver.

Mr. Johnson looked like a poodle in a fancy collar as he stood in the front of the bus and yapped at the two boys. They were giggling by the time he sat down in a huff. He wasn't crazy yet, but Cultus wouldn't stop until he was.

Cultus was Angie's cousin, although according to the Indian custom she called him her big brother. All cousins were just more brothers and sisters. Angie had so many of them she hadn't even seen them all. Some lived off the reservation; those she didn't know. Carysa was her only real sister.

4

She knew Cultus only too well. He was like her big brother, but she was usually ashamed of him. She wished it didn't have to be that way. He had a handsome round face, an easy smile, and he didn't wear his hair long. Angie liked that. She thought it was silly to draw attention to yourself by wearing Indian things to school, and she was glad that Cultus didn't embarrass her in that way. Katla kept her grandchildren clean and well-dressed, and Cultus wasn't as stupid as he pretended to be. He could have gotten along better at school if only he wanted to.

But Cultus didn't want to get along. And this last year it had been worse. Ever since starting high school he seemed to have a chip on his shoulder. He was a troublemaker, the kind that Katla said gave Indians a bad name. Katla told him to his face that he was going to end up in jail before he was even out of high school, just like that Paiute, Jackson Brooks, who took a gun to school and threatened to shoot the basketball coach.

The next stop was Lois's. She lived clear across the mesa and below the rimrock on the other side, near a place—as Katla told the story—where many years ago people shot green rocks from the cliffs with arrows. They used the rocks to dye buckskin, she explained. Lois lived a few miles beyond that place. And now as the bus drove beneath the green cliffs, Angie sat up in the seat in anticipation of her friend.

Lois stepped through the barbed wire fence just as the bus was slowing down to stop. She turned to hold the wires apart as her little brother, Willie, stepped through. They didn't have a cattle guard, and the wire gate at their driveway was too hard to open and close. They came through the fence every morning, and now the wires were so stretched that a horse or cow could come through it almost as easily as Lois did.

Lois boarded the bus with the same meek concentration, her eyes on her toes, but once she had passed the driver her face opened up in a smile for Angie. Lois had a definite way of sitting down on their shared seat. A habit. Angie, knowing the habit from experience, braced herself for a jolt that could send you farther into orbit than the traffic bump at the high school, if you didn't watch out for it.

"Hi," she said in English. And then she jumped a little, so that she could come down even harder. Then both of them slouched with their knees braced against the seat in front of them. "Did you get your Health done?" she asked.

"Yeah," Angie answered. "You?"

"Naw. My mom. You know. Anyway, can I see yours?" Angie produced her homework from her notebook. She knew Lois wouldn't have done her Math or her Science either, but Health was the only thing she cared enough about to do

6

the work. Miss Matson was their P.E. and Health teacher, and both girls agreed those were their favorite classes.

"I didn't get question number four. I don't get what all this 'poise' stuff is about. This chapter's s'posed to be about manners and . . ."

"That's okay," Lois interrupted. "I didn't get number four either. Can I have some paper?" Angie laughed. Lois just waited for the paper, and when Angie let her use her new Flair pen she got to work. It was going to be the kind of paper that would come back from Miss Matson saying, "Don't do your work on the bus." But Lois couldn't do her work at home. Her mom. Lois's mother was just like Angie's mother had been. That was the reason Angie lived with Katla, because her own mother had been an alcoholic, too. Angie had been small then, but she remembered those days with her mother very clearly. That was a bad time.

With Katla it was different. Katla was an Indian Shaker, and the one who rang the bell every Sunday in the Long-house. Angie remembered Katla giving testimony. She was talking about Angie's mother when she said, "Before the bell, all was sorrow in the Longhouse. We came here in sad-ness to bury our friends and family. All dead from drinking. Now sorrow lies behind the bell."

No one in Katla's house drank. And every one of the four

children she took care of, except Cultus, got his homework done. Angie's Katla was, as nearly as anybody could figure, seventy-four years old. She couldn't read or write or make change herself, but school was important at her house.

Lois's Katla was gone, so there was no one else for her. Oh, there was her little brother, Willie, but it seemed to Angie that she was the only one who could understand Lois. It was almost as if they talked a language of their own, not English and not Indian. The two of them could explain their problems to each other with just a word or two—"my mom"— and they could comfort each other with just a look.

So Angie didn't mind if Lois copied. Besides that, the bus was about the best time to do homework anyway. About all they had time for at home was dinner and sleep. Lois was focusing all of her efforts as she tried to write between corners and bumps in the road—cursive, backhand, and print, sometimes all in the same sentence. Finally she held the paper in front of her, looking it over with satisfaction. "Finished," she declared.

"Looks like three people did it," Angie said with a grin.

"Huh?"

But before Angie could explain to Lois how funny her handwriting looked, the paper vanished. It now occurred to Angie that the bus had been too quiet, and the reason for it was that Cultus and the rest were waiting for Lois to finish.

A window was pulled down and out went Lois's paper. Lois didn't take it well. She was standing in the aisle swearing at Cultus when Mr. Johnson stopped the bus right in the middle of the road. Lois sat back down.

"What's going on back there?" he shouted, getting out of his driver's seat fast and mad. Now it was really going to start, and with Lois this time.

"Them Cultus threw my Health paper out the window," Lois answered. She turned to Angie for support. "Isn't it, Angie, he threw it out?" Angie tried to look agreeably neutral.

"I never," yelled Cultus, outraged that he should be accused of such a thing. Then he nudged Grant Lokee with his elbow and snickered.

"Liar. You're ugly," Lois shouted back. Nothing else at hand, she grabbed Angie's notebook from her lap and threw it at Cultus. It hit Minnit Wahena instead, who said, "Ow—ouch!" dramatically as Cultus began to laugh. So Lois jumped at him, ready to fight.

"Stop it, you idiots," Johnson yelped, running to break it up. Lois's brother, Willie, stuck his foot out a little into the aisle, but it didn't work and Johnson ran on by without noticing. Lois was getting in her licks by the time he got to them, even if Cultus was laughing at her. Her fingerprints showed red on his brown cheeks where she'd slapped him.

9

"Stop it," the driver repeated at the top of his voice. He reached for Lois. Cultus was only a ninth grader, but he was big. He wasn't as tall as Johnson, of course. No Indian was as tall as Johnson, Angie thought. But Cultus was broad-shouldered and bulky with strength, like Indian men were, and Johnson was afraid of him. Everybody was afraid of him. So Johnson grabbed Lois instead of Cultus. He got hold of her arm and pushed her roughly into the seat next to Angie.

"Stop acting like animals," he shouted. Lois began to cry.

"He threw my Health paper out the window," she said, and for the sake of emphasis she added, "I worked all night on it." It didn't seem quite like a lie to Angie, under the circumstances.

"She was copying Angie," said Cultus in his own defense.

"You shut up," the driver said, turning on Cultus. "I've had just all I'm gonna take from you." Cultus hung his head, but not in shame. His face wore the expression he knew would make Johnson furious. Eyes blank. Lips not lifted in a smirk, but not pointed down at the corners in a frown either; somewhere just in between so that Johnson wasn't sure. Cultus was oblivious of him, as if he couldn't see Johnson, couldn't hear him. He looked like he might yawn. Johnson wasn't crazy yet, but he was getting close.

"I don't know what you think this is. Some kind of zoo or something?" he said hotly. "Well it ain't, and I don't have to put up with it. You seem to think you're going to drive me off this bus, but you're wrong. It's you who's going off this bus if this stupid baby stuff keeps up." Then he stopped. He seemed to be waiting, as if he expected a sign from Cultus that he would mend his ways. Cultus was stone. The blotches grew more red in the driver's face until Angie began to think he was going to turn polka-dotted.

"Don't you push me, or you'll lose," he said threateningly, pointing his finger into Cultus's face. Cultus seemed so oblivious to everything that it looked as if he'd stopped breathing. And Johnson was so mad he was shaking, but he seemed to think better of it and turned to go back to his driver's seat. Cultus lifted his eyes to watch his back. He'd won again.

Johnson no more than sat down when Grant Lokee shot him in the cheek with a rubber band. He hadn't even taken the brake off. And this time he got out of the seat with a scream. Angie groaned. Lois laughed.

"Who did that?" he shouted, his voice cracking with rage. He looked out into a busload of amused faces. "You, you animal," he said, looking back to Cultus. "Get up here." Still holding his cheek, he pointed to the doorstep. Cultus resumed his stoney look.

"Get up here," he repeated, quieter through clenched teeth, but angrier by the amount of fire in his eyes. Angie watched in terror as Johnson marched back and grabbed Cultus by the sleeve of his shirt. She was afraid of an open fist fight. But when Johnson pulled on the sleeve, Cultus didn't resist.

He didn't give, either. The sleeve tore.

Cultus looked at his shoulder where the seam was ripped, then at Johnson. When Cultus stood, Johnson backed toward the front of the bus. This time Willie's foot managed to make Johnson stumble a little, but again he didn't seem to notice. Cultus walked with quiet dignity to the front of the bus and sat down on the step.

As often as this sort of thing happened with Cultus, she was always a little stunned by it. And it was worse, Angie reflected, when it happened on the first part of the ride. When these outbursts happened before they let the little kids off in Red Salmon, they saw it all—ate it all up for breakfast and took Cultus's bellyache off the bus with them. Angie didn't like it. Carysa was only in the second grade and already she was beginning to act ornery like Cultus. Of course, Carysa saw Cultus all the time at home, but he was different then. Not really bad. Lazy maybe, but not bad, and at home he played with Carysa like a big brother.

Today, when the bus stopped in Red Salmon to let the little kids off, Cultus stood in the doorway to let them by. When Carysa went by him she said something that made him laugh; whatever it was, Angie wanted to pop her a good one for it.

At least the stop in Red Salmon changed Lois's mood. She sulked instead of swore.

"You want to look at my Health again?" Angie offered.

"Naw." Lois was carefully drawing elaborate initials onto the backs of both hands with Angie's Flair pen. There were Angie's initials and Lois's initials with plus signs in between. Angie made conversation.

"Your dress finished yet?"

"Naw. My mom was in there all night." With a nod of her head, Lois indicated the Pioneer. They were just over the boundary of the reservation, and the Pioneer was the first tavern. It was so close to the boundary that people could stand in the parking lot and lob beer bottles onto Indian land.

"It would really be neat if both of us had new buffalo dresses this year," she went on. "Think you'll have to wear a wing dress again?"

Buffalo dresses! Angie thought with a thrill about dancing in the Longhouse in a skin dress. The fact that a family went to the expense and work to make fancy Indian clothes said something important to everyone. Katla explained that Angie was only going to get her new dress when she accepted the responsibilities of keeping the Indian ways. Angie didn't care much about all that. What Angie cared about was having a dress like Lois's, and she would put up with Katla's old-fashioned ideas to get it if she had to.

"It's all cut out," Lois answered, looking up from the artwork in progress on the backs of her hands. "All she needs to do is put it together. Then there's the fringe. But she said that if she has time she'll put shells on the shoulders like Marta's."

"Me too," Angie said. "I mean, I want mine to look like Marta's too. Marta's gonna make another one, though, so it depends. Katla will probably work on hers first." Katla always did that, worked on Marta's stuff first. She was the oldest—Cultus's real sister—so maybe it was right. Besides, Marta was supposed to be about the best girl dancer on the reservation. For somebody so dumb, Angie thought, Marta sure always did things right.

"That's why Marta always wins the dance contest," Lois said. "'Cause your Katla always makes the best Indian clothes at the Powwow." Angie knew what she meant. The women's dances weren't exactly interesting to watch. They weren't much more than a shuffle. The richness of the costumes mattered as much as the dancing, and Marta's beads and shawls and dresses—everything—were the very best.

"Marta always does what Katla wants her to do." Angie

spoke behind her hand because Marta was sitting two seats in front of them. "She does what everybody wants her to do. She's dumb. She even tries to talk Indian at home because Katla likes it." And they both laughed.

"Ugh ugh ugh ugh," Lois carried on in a silly imitation of Indian language. Both snickered behind Marta.

"I can't understand a word of it," Lois stated.

"Me neither," Angie lied. She had to understand it, of course, because Katla spoke only Indian at home. Angie didn't speak it. She would answer Katla in English. But she certainly could understand it.

"Did I ever tell you about the time Marta got in trouble at school for talkin' Indian?" Angie grew confidential as she started to tell the story.

"Uh uh," Lois said. She had actually heard it and Angie knew that. But it was a good story, and it showed how stupid Marta was.

"Well, you know that Mr. Miller who teaches Chemistry?"

"What did she wanta take Chemistry for?" Lois interrupted immediately. It was part of the formula for the story, always told with the same interruptions in the same places.

"I don't know. That's the kind of dummy Marta is. Anyway, she must have liked them Mr. Miller because one day she said good-bye to him in Indian, however you say that.

And them Miller thought she was cussin' at him or something. He sent her to the office." Both girls shook their heads in shared disbelief that Marta—anyone—could be so simple.

As they neared Baker, the girls grew silent again. The highway became Main Street. Most of the businesses were gas stations, but Angie took it all in with the interest of a visitor. The bus turned between the Dairy Queen and the Bank of Oregon and drove through four blocks of houses. They had lawns. The trees in the yards weren't junipers. The cars in the driveways were newer. And at the end of the street was the traffic bump. Like a cattle guard, Angie thought. It announced to her backside the beginning of the school grounds. They were there.

When the bus stopped, Johnson was the first off, ordering Cultus to follow him. "We're going to see Mr. McGilvra," he announced. They walked toward the office door.

Angie and Lois went to school in the same building. The junior high and the high school were connected, but the girls had their own entrance into the junior high wing. They watched Cultus walk behind Johnson before going into their part of the building.

"Hey Cultus!" Lois yelled after him.

He turned, smiling, and raised his hand in the familiar V-for-victory sign. The girls laughed back and returned the sign before turning to enter the school.

16

2

Cultus had been suspended from the bus for a week, but they couldn't leave him stranded. He had to ride the bus home before he could be suspended from it. He sat smugly in his place.

"What happened, Cultus? Did them McGilvra give you a hack?" Lois teased with her voice but there was admiration in her eyes. Angie wouldn't have dared ask that question.

"Naw. He's too chicken. He knows he better not try it," Cultus said with menace in his voice. Angie wondered if he was lying. McGilvra, the principal, was a mousey little man who seemed to be in his office and on the telephone most of the time. Angie had never seen him angry—she'd hardly seen him at all—but she knew that he gave some of the boys hacks with a paddle that he kept in his office.

"What did he say?"

"Oh, the same old stuff he always says. He read something to me from that handbook thing just like he always does."

17

"Is that all?"

"Yeah. What of it?" Cultus said, threateningly. "You calling me a liar or something?"

"No. I only . . ." Lois faltered and Angie nudged her to keep her quiet. Lois didn't know Cultus well enough to know when he was covering something up.

The girls scrunched themselves up in their seat, getting out of sight. "Wow, I was just trying to talk to him," Lois said. "Why'd he blow up like that?"

"Because McGilvra gave him a hack, that's why," Angie answered.

Cultus was in a pout the rest of the way home, but it was a wild ride all the same. Johnson didn't seem quite so anxious to encounter the whole busload of them over each spitwad or insult or slap. Sally Mitchell poured half a bottle of orange pop into Dorothy Winisha's lap. Ian Wahena made Willie cry when he called him a little woman (Willie still wore braids). Willie punched him and made his nose bleed. Sammy Bruce, known among his friends as Bruce the Goose, applied his thumb to everyone smaller than he was if they had to pass him to get off the bus. And Johnson drove. In his mirror, Angie could see that the wrinkle in his brow was so deep his forehead was almost split clear in half. He didn't look very happy now that he'd kicked Cultus off the bus. It wasn't going to be easy telling Katla.

18

Johnson had to give her the bus slip himself. There were no telephones in Angie's remote end of the reservation, so the principal couldn't tell her about it. He wasn't likely to drive forty-nine miles one-way to deliver a bus slip. And Johnson couldn't just hand it to Cultus as he got off the bus and expect the slip to make it a half mile up the road to the cabin. It would end up the same place report cards did.

Because the bus couldn't make the turn into their driveway, Johnson parked it right on the road and left the light flashing. He took the keys with him, thinking, perhaps, that one of the Winisha or Mitchell kids might steal the bus. And he put the block under a front wheel to keep it from rolling down the hill and into Badger Creek all by itself. Before leaving the bus, Johnson wagged his finger and threatened the children who were waiting to "behave or else."

"All right, come on," he said to the four of them. He wouldn't let them get off until he was ready to go, but as soon as they hit the ground Carysa took off like a rabbit. She was like that about everything— always the first to tell Katla, a little tattletale.

The walk up the rutted road was faster and quieter than Angie enjoyed. No one talked. They just took long, fast steps and kicked up a lot of dust. Angie felt sweaty and out of breath, but she didn't want to be left behind.

Katla was there to meet them when they reached the

shapeless section of bare dirt they called the front yard. Carysa stood on the porch behind Katla, looking ready to defend the door from any intrusion.

"How you go, mister?" she said by way of greeting him. Katla was short, maybe five feet tall, and round. She stood powerfully, though, as solid a natural feature of the prairie as the deep-rooted junipers and the persistent sage. She was as firm as rimrock in her high moccasins. They came up her calves and disappeared beneath the hem of her wing dress just below the knees. Arms folded beneath her red shawl, and with a bright yellow handkerchief pulled tightly over her hair, she looked just as she always did to Angie, but she must have presented a formidable appearance to Johnson. He spoke to the ground in front of his feet.

"I'm sorry to trouble you with this again," he started, "but this time Cultus has gone too far. He gave me so much trouble on the bus this morning that I had to take him to the principal." He sounded as if he were apologizing to her for it, Angie thought.

Katla seemed to consider this awhile, her eyes staring straight into Johnson. Angie watched her face. Its Indian features were exaggerated by her age. It was rounded, but all the softness was gone out of it, as if it had been crudely chiseled from wood, then left to dry so that deep cracks ran through her cheeks. It didn't move.

20

"What he done?" The question finally came. She didn't shift her eyes. They continued to cut into Johnson and he squirmed.

"Well, lots of things," Johnson replied, lifting his gaze to a place above Katla's head, then dropping it once again. Why won't whites look you in the eyes? Angie asked herself. Then she remembered Cultus, and the way he could look at nothing almost forever. She could do it, too.

"For instance, yesterday he was spitting chewing tobacco all over the floor. And today he started a fight with a seventh-grade girl." It sounded almost silly to Angie, as if Cultus hadn't done much at all. Katla didn't look too shocked by it, and Angie wondered if she would think Cultus was in trouble for nothing. But she would know Cultus better than that.

"So I kicked him off the bus. For a week."

"What?" Katla said it immediately, as if that surprised her, although the old coyote had to know. Carysa would have told her. "You kicked him off them bus! What he done that's all that bad?" Her eyes were even sharper as she said this, but her face still didn't move.

"He tore my shirt," Cultus said defensively. Katla's eyes flashed at him. Her look told him to shut up, and he shook his head helplessly and looked away.

"I told you what he did," Johnson said. "And if he's gonna act like that, I don't want him on my bus. And I don't have to take him either. Riding the bus ain't a right, you know. It's a privilege." Angie made a face. How many times had she heard that before? "If it don't stop, he's gonna have to find another way to get to school, permanent. I've had it."

Now Katla's face changed. "What I'm supposed to do, bus driver?" she asked, disgusted. "I'm a old woman. Seventy-four years old. He won't get me firewood. See that pile over there?" She nodded to the pile of wood their Uncle Dan had dumped from his pickup. "He won't even carry it as far as the porch. He won't get water. I ask him get me something, he sits there. You think I can whip him? When there was Whipman, not just at Powwow but all the time Whipman, Indian kids don't act like this. Whip hang on the wall all the time and watch. When Whipman come, whip tell him who been bad.

"Then Whipman say, 'Open your heart, love.' And he make them dance, the kids. And then Whipman hit them all, all kids, parents, old people like me all gets whipped. Now no more Whipman, and Indian kids all bad. Maybe you need Whipman on them bus. Why don't you whip all them kids?" Katla finished with another nod that included Angie, Marta, and Cultus.

"I can't do that!" Johnson denied that responsibility with force. "I'd get fired if I did," he explained. "A bus driver can't do that."

22

"Well, what I'm supposed to do with him, mister bus driver? I'm a old woman, seventy-four years old. I can't drive a car. I can't take him to school. You tell me, what I'm supposed to do?"

"I don't know," Johnson admitted. Angie thought he was going to give in and say it was okay for Cultus to ride the bus on Monday. He didn't. Johnson really was tougher than most. He didn't say anything.

"You think I want that lazy boy home with me all day?" Katla asked. "That how he wants it. You look at this boy now." Johnson did as he was told. Angie almost laughed. "You know he hates them school. Much as I know it, you know it. You givin' him just how he wants it."

"Well he can't stay out of school just 'cause he gets kicked off the bus," Johnson said. "If he don't go to school, the truant officer will be after you."

"What I'm supposed to do then? I'm a old woman. I can't drive. I can't read. Got no phone. I knows how to write two words, when I writes my name."

"I guess you'll have to talk to the principal about it then. I can't help you."

"How I'm supposed to talk to them McGilvra?"

"I don't know," Johnson said. "I got to get back to my bus. I'm late enough already, and those Winisha kids probably tore the bus to pieces by now. It wouldn't take much," he added indistinctly. Katla stood staring him right in the face, firm and disgusted. Johnson seemed to be searching his mind to see if there was anything left to say. There wasn't. He turned and walked down the driveway. He turned again after a few steps, not really looking back and still walking. "See you," he said weakly.

Angie couldn't tell what Katla was going to do by looking at her. The children all watched to see what was going to happen. Once she'd hit Cultus with a piece of firewood and he'd given her a black eye for it, his own Katla. All of them had cried with her when Cultus ran away. He had hitch-hiked to Uncle Dan's, who beat him to a pulp before bringing him home the same day.

Katla just looked at them. Her eyes went from one to another, searingly, and Angie cringed when they landed on her. Why was Katla mad at her—at all of them?

Katla spat in the dust in front of the three children, turned, and walked heavily into the cabin in her buckskin moccasins. Cultus walked off down the road.

Angie guessed that Katla went into the bedroom to lie down. There wouldn't be any dinner tonight, unless maybe she and Marta fixed it. She could picture Katla lying on her back in bed staring up at the ceiling the way she always did when something like this happened.

Angie went to the smokehouse and carried in the wood

without having to be told to do it tonight. It was a pleasant walk up behind the cabin to the smokehouse; the junipers were thicker, the air fragrant with the smell of the trees and horses and smoke, too. The horses liked the shade of the trees so much that the ground around them was bare in circles like in an orchard. No grass could grow at the base of the trees because the horses were always there.

She carried in an armload of small pieces. Juniper wood. The meat hanging in the smokehouse had an irresistible smell. She picked off a few strips of the dried venison and chewed on one as she spread the coals evenly beneath the racks, holding the rake in one hand and the jerky in the other. Then, chewing on jerky, she walked back to the cabin.

She stopped on the way to look for the lark. She could hear it, somewhere in the clumps of cheat grass between the trees. She couldn't see it. Katla told them that the lark always told the future. If you listened carefully enough, it would tell it to you, but only in Indian. The lark sounded mournful, and she couldn't see it.

Angie went back to the cabin and sat on the porch, watching their road. Funny, she thought. Why should she worry about where he was, after all the trouble he caused everybody? But it was dark by the time she knew Cultus wasn't coming home that night, and she went in to bed.

3

Every Saturday morning Angie's Uncle Dan took them all into Red Salmon. They had only one day to do a whole week's business, so most of Saturday was spent at the store.

Stacey's was one of those places that had everything. In the main part there were canned foods, fresh produce, a butcher shop that would cut up deer and elk too, coolers of pop but no beer, a counter that sold beads and buckskin and other Indian goods, a shelf with automotive supplies and another with clothes like T-shirts that said "American Indian—The Real Thing," and more. Into one back corner was tucked the post office where everyone on the reservation had a box. In the other back corner a door led to the "museum," which held a collection of arrow tips and scrapers and beadwork and rifles, a rolled teepee, dusty war bonnets, a stuffed buffalo head, and a thousand other things—all Indian, all old, all neglected.

This was where Katla did her shopping, except on those

rare occasions when she ventured as far as Baker. But Stacey's was even more than a store, a post office, and a museum. The ugly green, windowless building was built on a hill, so that when you drove around back there was another layer. This was the Laundromat. At the back of the Laundromat were showers. For ten cents the showers would run hot water for ten minutes. Cold showers were free.

When Uncle Dan drove up with Cultus in the cab of his pickup, Katla was mad. It wasn't a surprise; she knew he'd be with his uncle because there was no place else for him to go. She was mad because she knew Dan would be in league with Cultus against her.

Of the thirty-odd children, grandchildren, nieces, nephews, and strays that Katla had raised, Dan was one of the more successful products. He had a job with the tribe. He went to the Longhouse every Sunday. He kept them supplied with salmon and deer, and since he was the only one who could drive, they depended upon him for just about everything else, too.

That's not to say, however, that Katla would admit that he was perfect. In fact, Katla was more inclined to bring up his shortcomings, which she would sum up with one short sentence: "He's stupid."

He wasn't, of course. He wasn't nearly so ignorant as he was proud, and what she meant by that was that Dan didn't have much schooling. He didn't think it was a good thing to learn too much of what the white man had to offer. Katla felt he was a bad influence on Cultus because he agreed with the boy about school.

Cultus didn't come into the cabin. He stayed in the pickup while they got ready, stuffing the dirty clothes into plastic bags. The girls tied handkerchiefs over their heads, the way Katla always did; it was a windy ride in the back of the pickup, and no matter how tight one's braids were, hair flew into your eyes and mouth unless you tied it down with a handkerchief. There were trips to the outhouse. Returnable bottles were gathered. Coats located. When everybody was ready, finally, Cultus tried to escape from the cab to join the girls in the back. He was ordered to stay where he was, and they had hardly reached the paved road before the argument started.

Angie sat right under the back window. That was the place most sheltered from the wind, but she really sat there so she could listen. Katla was talking Indian, hard to hear over the noise of the road. Indian language isn't loud; it's almost whispered. Angie could hear Dan and Cultus, but she had to wait until Katla got really mad before she could understand what she was saying.

"No, you can't quit school," Katla said loud enough.

28

"Why not? They don't want me there. They'd be glad if I quit," Cultus returned in English.

"You can't quit school," Katla repeated.

"You didn't care so much when I quit," Dan said with resentment in his voice. "Why shouldn't he quit? He'd be better off getting a job on the reservation than learning how to read and write like a white man. You sure didn't make such a fuss over me."

"That was different," Katla reasoned. "That was boarding school. That was like somebody had stolen my children from me."

"How's that different from now?" Cultus insisted. "Every day that bus comes and takes me off the reservation. That's stealing, ain't it?"

"You don't know what you're talking about!" Dan seemed to be forgetting whose side he was on. "They didn't have no school bus to bring me home every night in them days. It was on the reservation, sure, but it's still thirty-two miles to Red Salmon so I didn't exactly walk home for lunch every day. And no matter how bad that Baker school is, it ain't nowhere near so bad as that federal prison—'cause that's just what it was to us, that boarding school."

"They would come home in the summer and tell me about that school," Katla said with a mixture of bitterness and sorrow in her voice, "and what they told me just made me sad inside. But there was nothing we could do about it. So finally I just let you stay home, Dan. But things are different now with this school. It's not like they steal my kids anymore."

"So things are different!" Dan was back on Cultus's team. "I never done so bad. I got a job. An Indian job. I don't have to go into Baker every day to work in a white man's shoe store like Gene Winam and them others. So things are different. So what? Cultus could do what I done and still make out all right."

"Yeah. You even got a hill named after you, you turned out so smart," Katla said sarcastically. Angie, in the back of the truck, grinned in anticipation of the story Katla was about to tell. She always told this story to prove how stupid Dan was. It didn't prove anything, but it was funny to see how furious it made Dan when she told it.

"Yessir. You're so smart they named a hill after you," Katla repeated for effect. "They call it The Place-Where-Dan-Jumps-Off in your honor."

"That could've happened to anybody," Dan said loudly. "The brake . . ."

"Let me tell you about your Uncle Dan's good job, Cultus," she continued.

"He's heard it before," Dan cried out.

"Your Uncle Dan, he works for the forestry," she went on, ignoring him. "Now, he's not just a logger. No sir. He works for the tribe. He's a big shot. He prevents fires."

"Aw, shut up!" he said, but she wouldn't, of course. It really wasn't fair, Angie reflected. But it was funny.

"Now I gave your uncle the Indian name, Bear-Who-Stands, in the Longhouse when he was a boy. He was always such a big boy. Almost like you, Cultus, but even bigger when he was your age. But I think I named him wrong. I should have named him Smokey Bear." Katla was the only one inside the cab who laughed.

"Cut it out!"

"Let me tell you about Smokey Bear's job. You see all these signs all over the reservation? What do they say, Cultus? You know I can't read them. Well, that's your Uncle Dan's good job. He puts up some of these signs every summer. The rest of the time he drives around in a fire truck. Maybe he drinks a little beer at the boundary. Sometimes he takes a little nap in the Longhouse when he's supposed to be cleaning the floors. Sometimes he even works through his lunch hour, if he can find some loggers to play stick game. Sometimes he shoots a deer, sometimes he . . ."

"You don't have any idea what I do," said Dan, "so why don't you shut up about it?"

"So once your Uncle Smokey Bear gets to a fire first, all

by himself, way up in the mountains. He jumps out of his truck and grabs the hose. But your smart Uncle Dan, the one who didn't have to go to school to get such a good job, I guess he didn't stop the truck so good. There he is holding onto the hose when the fire truck just up and jumps off the road behind him. Then it falls off a cliff and your Uncle Dan has to run away from the fire. That's your smart Uncle Dan. Now they call that hill The-Place-Where-Dan-Jumps-Off. It's a good place to pick berries because there aren't any trees on that hill anymore."

"The brake failed. I stopped it just like I was supposed to. I've told you that before. It could've happened to anybody."

Cultus, who must have felt they were forgetting his problem, said, "Well, what am I supposed to do then?" He was beginning to sound desperate.

"Dan, you take him to school next week," Katla said. There wasn't a trace of request in this. It was an order.

"But I have to . . ." Dan started to protest.

"You're going to be hunting for the Longhouse and getting ready for the Powwow. Don't tell me you have to go to work!"

Cultus, who obviously wasn't getting his way—he wasn't even getting them to pay attention to him—finally started to have a real fit. "You just don't understand," he objected. "Nobody understands me. I hate that place. It's their place.

They don't know anything about us except that we're not like them. We look different. And we live in a place they can't understand. They never even been over the boundary to find out what it's like. To them this reservation is like a jail or a hospital. It's like we're wrong or sick and they're going to fix us."

"Dan, take us to Baker," Katla said when Cultus had finished.

"I told you I got to work on Monday."

"I mean now. Today."

"Aw fer . . . what in the world for?" he complained.

"I'm going to do what that driver told me to do," she explained. "I'm going to go talk to McGilvra."

Katla never went to parent-teacher conferences. She was afraid of teachers, though she always said she couldn't go to conferences because "I don't talk that English no good." Angie didn't believe she spoke it half so bad as she wanted everybody to think she did.

Katla wouldn't go to conferences, but here she was, trying to see the principal on Saturday morning. She was ready to talk. Now. That's what the whites meant by "Indian time." Angie had heard them say Indians were late for everything, but she wondered how whites could expect anyone to do anything until they were ready.

Baker was a small town. The sign at the city limits said

"Population 2,490." You couldn't live forty-nine miles from the place without knowing where the principal of the high school lived. Dan drove right to his house. Angie wanted to lie down in the back of the pickup and hide, and she would have, but it might just make her look more foolish than she already did.

Katla got out of the truck and said, "Come with me, Angie." She was afraid to go alone.

"What? Oh no-o-o," Angie groaned. "Why not take Marta?" she pleaded. Marta slugged her.

"Come on. Get out of there. Now!" Katla ordered. She wouldn't go anywhere without one of them. To translate, she always said, which might have been true at Stacey's because she couldn't make change. But this time it was because she was scared.

Angie felt that every eye on the block was watching her as she climbed out of the pickup. All those white people must be thinking, What are *they* doing here? She followed Katla up the walk.

At the door Katla knocked, although there was a doorbell. Angie stared hard into the daffodils by the front step, listening to her own heart making more noise than Katla was, banging on the door. There were footsteps. The door opened, and a woman with a friendly smile and puzzled eyes asked, "Yes? May I help you?"

34

"I want to talk them McGilvra," Katla said, trying not to appear shy. Anger was about the easiest way to cover it up, so she sounded angry.

"I'm sorry," the woman apologized evenly. "Mr. McGilvra is not at home. Is there anything I can do? I'm Mrs. McGilvra."

Angie was afraid Katla might tell her the whole story. She did something worse, Angie thought. "Where is he, then?" Katla insisted. **2087236**

"I'm afraid he can't be reached this weekend. He'll be in his office on Monday."

Katla was offended by the way the woman answered, or maybe she didn't believe her. "Why don't he want to talk to me?" she asked. Angie was dying of shame. They'd all be sorry when they had to pick her body up out of the daffodils.

"That's not it at all. If he were home, I'm sure he would be happy to talk with you."

Katla gave up. "All right," she said, and rudely turned to walk back to the pickup. She climbed up and slammed the door behind her. Angie stole looks up and down the street. She didn't see anyone, but she was sure they were watching, laughing at them. The shame of it didn't end after they drove away. Angie could still feel those eyes on her.

As if trying to make up for the morning, Katla bought them all something in the department store in Baker: a motorcycle T-shirt for Carysa, blouses that matched for Marta and Angie, two pairs of pants for Cultus that weren't blue jeans and that he said he wouldn't wear, a straw cowboy hat for Dan, and popcorn for everyone. For herself, Katla bought a bright, slippery scarf with a map of Oregon on it to wear as a head cloth. She also bought beads in Baker instead of at Stacey's, enough to decorate the buckskin gloves and moccasins she would auction at the Longhouse in the morning and some extra. She promised to bead eagles on Angie's and Marta's leggin's before the Powwow if she had time.

The time to work on the leggin's didn't come that weekend. That evening Katla finished the items she would auction. With her bead basket open in front of her on the table, she sat hunchbacked, concentrating on her work in the failing light of evening. This was work she would sell to raise money for the Powwow Committee, to pay the prize money and the drummers and to buy gifts. The old women worked months to raise the money—first prize for the men's war dance was five hundred dollars. That took a lot of beading, but Katla's was always perfect, always cut glass and no plastic.

"You should learn to do this, Angie," Katla said to her. Angie was playing jacks on the floor. "I won't always be here to teach you."

"I don't want to learn to do it," Angie replied nastily. Katla was hurt, she could see, and she was glad. Angie could still feel the shame of what Katla had done that morning.

"Then you go get some water and heat it to do the dishes," Katla said, the hurt sounding in her voice. Angie, leaving the jacks on the floor, walked out onto the porch. She didn't take the bucket with her and she didn't pump the water. Obstinate and bored, she leaned against a post on the porch and watched the sun go down behind the high Cascades.

She drew a hopscotch court in the area of light cast from the cabin window and began to play, throwing her string of yellow beads. It felt fine, the dry dirt powdering her bare feet with each jump, cool and clean-feeling dust between her toes. She played until Cultus, on his way back from doing her chores for her in the smokehouse, dragged his feet over the lines she'd drawn.

After that she sat on the porch, her feet in the cool dirt. She drew pictures in the dust with her finger for a while, mostly hearts pierced with arrows. "Angie + Lois," she wrote in them. She was bored with it, so she wrote a nasty word. She was still bored, and she smoothed the dirt out with her feet and just sat.

She sat for the longest time, just thinking about nothing in particular, and listening to Spilyay, the coyote, up on the hill. His call sounded like the musical saw the blind man played each year at the All-Indian Rodeo in Baker. The moon dropped its spare change into his cup.

4

Angie was tired Sunday morning. Katla sent her out to the pump to wash in the cold water. "It's the Indian way, just like the old days," Katla always said, but Angie just couldn't bring herself to do it. Cultus, who bragged about sweating with Uncle Dan, splashed his face and chest and arms. When the cold water touched him, he screamed as if he had just come out of a sweathouse and someone had thrown a bucket of cold water on him. Angie shuddered, listening. The thought of that cold water touching her skin was as prickly as the thought of ticks or spiders crawling on her. She didn't even wash the corners of her eyes.

Katla made fried bread for them as they dressed. She spread the dough on her fingertips and dropped each piece delicately into the pan of hot fat. The fat was so hot on top of the wood stove that it sizzled when the dough fell into it. The room was filled with the heavy, greasy smell that Angie associated with the taste of the bread. She liked it hot, sticky, and dripping with butter. The taste was so simple and right that she seldom put honey or sugar or jam on the bread. Dressing, they ate in turns, as soon as each piece came steaming from the pan of fat.

Angie helped Carysa dress. Their Indian clothes were kept in boxes beneath the bed they shared. As she pulled each piece of clothing from the box, the Indian word for it popped into her mind. She pushed it down, only to have another pop up somewhere else, like a diving duck coming up for air.

"*Mtichni pama.* No—underdress!" she corrected. "*K'peep* —sounds like what a chicken with a cold would say, that word for wing dress."

Her belt for Sunday wasn't beaded. It was crocheted, not as fancy as the beaded belt which had been her mother's. She wore that belt only at Powwows.

Dan drove up. He waited patiently, eating bread, until they were ready. The girls and Katla were dressed similarly, although in different colors and prints. The wing dresses were bright and billowy, pulled in at the waist with a belt. The girls wore moccasins that came up only to their ankles, and knee socks covered their legs between ankle and hem. Katla's moccasins were higher. All wore strings of beads around their necks and fur braid ties. With prayer shawls folded over their arms, and rubber overshoes on their feet to protect their moccasins, they paraded out to take their places in Dan's pickup.

Katla was always first to get to the Longhouse on Sunday. Before other Sunday worshipers arrived, she would turn the heat up, Dan would run a broom quickly over the floor, and the rest of them would do whatever housekeeping chores were necessary to get the building ready. There was work to be done, but not so much that Angie couldn't find time for herself.

The Longhouse had rest rooms with hot water and flush toilets. Angie's procrastination at the pump paid off as she washed her face in warm water. She congratulated herself as she remembered the scene Cultus made at the pump that morning.

The thought came to her that boys were silly to struggle so. Cultus at the pump was just like at school when the Indian boys would link arms and crash through the halls, hoping to bump into somebody and start a fight; or the way they pushed to the front of the line; or the way they proved how tough they were by being crude and pretending to be stupid.

She remembered another time Cultus had gone to the principal's office. She had actually only heard about it from Minnit Wahena, who was in Cultus's English class, but she

40

knew it was true because it sounded just like Cultus.

Mr. Loomis, the English teacher, was new that year. The interesting thing about Mr. Loomis was his car. It wasn't the kind of car Angie would ever have wanted, but it must have been fun to ride in. It was a cute little green sports car, and on warm days in the fall Mr. Loomis had driven it to school with the top down. Other than that, Mr. Loomis was just another high school teacher as far as Angie was concerned.

The way Minnit told the story, Mr. Loomis had assigned something for the class to read, and Cultus hadn't done it. Mr. Loomis was trying to make an example of Cultus by asking him questions that he knew Cultus couldn't answer. Cultus just sat there with a blank look on his face, Minnit said. Finally, Mr. Loomis lost his temper and said Cultus was just like a cigar-store Indian.

Later Mr. Loomis's car was scraped by a bottle opener down both sides, and everybody knew who had done it even if they couldn't prove it. Then McGilvra gave Cultus a hack with his paddle—not so much because of the damage he did to Mr. Loomis's car, but because he refused to apologize for it.

It was that kind of bull-headedness that made Cultus seem so unfathomable to Angie. As she felt the warm water on her face, Angie thought how much easier it was just to get along.

Marta came into the rest room, and Angie couldn't resist the urge to share her new wisdom. She felt she had everything figured out this morning.

"Isn't it, Marta, boys are crazy? Like Cultus this morning, bellowing like a bull, when he could have waited and used hot water. Boys are all too stupid!"

"Yeah, well you ain't all that smart yourself, Angie," she said. She stood looking at the mirror over Angie's shoulder as she considered her braid ties.

"What do you mean by that?" Angie asked. Marta's look changed to concern as their eyes met through the mirror.

"Angie, Katla's upset because you're not speaking Indian at home. And she knows the way you and Lois make fun of Indian language. I guess I told her about that. But there are other things, too. Like with the Powwow coming up so soon. You don't even care enough about it to tell Katla what you want beaded on your dress, let alone help her with it. I know you're worried about Cultus, but it's getting so that you're as bad, only different."

With that she looked sharply down. It was the way, having said too much, and she left.

"Ugh, ugh, ugh," Angie whispered to the mirror. She was shocked that Katla knew about that.

The worship service started after the drummers took their places. They sat in a row, then stood to play their hand drums. This was unlike the drummers at the Powwows, who sat while drumming in a circle around one big war drum. Katla was in her place, bell in hand, at one end of the drummers, and as soon as the music started Angie went out onto the floor.

She spread her shawl carefully over her shoulders and across in front of her so that she could hold it closed with one hand. She held a cluster of eagle feathers—genuine ones because Katla wouldn't settle for less—in her hand. Then, before taking her place among the dancers, she had to turn around in one complete circle to the left. Angie didn't know why, but she always had to do this, whether joining or leaving the dancers. If she forgot, Katla would remember and get mad.

Once among the dancers, Angie talked quietly with her neighbors until the drummers stood, holding their hand drums high, as a signal for the beginning of each song. They sang in Indian, in the same high-pitched voice they used for tribal dances, but their songs on Sunday were about the Christian God.

The dance was always the same. Angie was part of a big circle. On her side were women, and facing them the men made up the other half of it across the room. When the drummers struck their drums, the whole room throbbed, and the dancers bent at the knee, dipping in rhythm to the beat.

43

Angie fanned her feathers in a way that copied the ringing of the bell. Others had feathers, too. Those without them rocked their empty hands with the same movement. They stood in one place, dipping to the drums until the bell rang loudly through the music.

At this signal, the circle shuffled to the right, the dancers stepping to the side with energy and bringing their left foot up with a slide. Halfway around the floor they stopped, bending at the knee again in one place and fanning their feathers. When the bell pierced the music a second time, the dancers shuffled around to their starting positions, completing their turn around the floor. The bell, the drumming, the singing, rose to a fever pitch. Sometimes Katla, ringing, became so excited that she jumped powerfully into the air. Then the music just wound down and stopped. The drummers sat. That song was over.

While the drummers sat, the dancers stood in their places, talking quietly with their neighbors. In a minute or two the drummers would stand, and it would start all over again. There were seven songs before a break, and seven sevens before each meal. Angie was expected to dance them all. So, although Angie looked forward to Sundays at the Longhouse because they were a chance to spend some time with Lois, their time together didn't amount to much. Angie was expected to dance, and Lois helped her mother, who was one of the Sunday cooks. Sometimes Lois danced, and they were able to talk a little then, but not seriously because it just wasn't the right place. Usually they had to wait until after the worship service was over.

Lois came into the Longhouse in the middle of the second seven. Her mother didn't look good, but Lois, in her wing dress, smiled and lifted her hand in a carefree wave to Angie.

She danced all seven sevens before talking with Lois. The Longhouse was more crowded than usual because of the nearness to Powwow. The benches were full of hungry dancers, and there was so much to be done in the kitchen that Lois didn't get to dance. Angie had her first chance to say hello to her friend when the meal was served.

"I've got something to tell you," Angie whispered to her when she was able. "I can't tell you about it now," she said, "but we went to Baker yesterday."

"We didn't go nowhere," Lois grumped in response. She was filling paper cups with water from a pitcher. Not exactly filling them—only about half full. The water was part of the prayer before the meal. "Except the Pioneer," she said. "Me and Willie had to stay in the car all day. What'd you do in them Baker?"

"That's what I got to tell you. It's just crazy." Angie almost told her about it then and there because Lois didn't seem very interested. It's harder to keep a secret when no one seems to want to know it, Angie discovered, but she held out. "I can't tell you here. Meet you later, okay? When you're finished in the kitchen."

"Yeah, okay, if my mom don't make me wash the dishes. Maybe when they're having the auction. I gotta go bring out the food now." Lois seemed tired.

Angie ate with her family. Folding tables had been set up so that they could eat from the Longhouse benches. It was something like having a seat assigned on the bus, since every family had their own place on the bench. No one made them sit in the same place every Sunday. They just did.

The meal began after the prayer. Everyone was forbidden to taste the food until the word *chush* was pronounced by the person—usually Katla—who said the prayer. The word meant, simply, drink. It was the same after the meal. No one left the tables to clear away the dishes until water was drunk from the paper cups.

The food was there in plenty, but the meal wasn't fancy. All the best food was saved for the Powwow. The rest of the time the food at the Longhouse was like leftovers. The salmon wasn't baked fresh, it was dried. The corn had been dried, too, and then boiled. The roots were "red"—that is, prepared the same way as the corn. Everything was dried so it would keep. The vegetables were pretty chewy.

Also to choose from were venison with dumplings, fried

bread, frozen huckleberries, and cupcakes. At first Angie put only a little salmon and four cupcakes on her plate. Katla made her take berries and roots, too, but let her keep the cupcakes.

Seven sevens and another meal later, the girls were free at last. This was why Sundays were special for Angie, this time with Lois. After the tables were cleared away and the auction had started, the girls tried to find a place just right for sharing secrets. The best place was always in the parking lot.

It felt like rain so the girls sat in Lois's car, the two of them in the front seat with their legs pulled up under them, wrinkling their dresses. Angie told Lois about going up to McGilvra's door. Lois didn't seem to care, and the windows were steaming up with their small talk when Lois's voice became serious.

"Do you think Cultus would like my hair short?" she asked, holding her face in front of the mirror on the dashboard. Something in the way their eyes met as Lois untied her braids reminded Angie of her talk with Marta in the bathroom that morning. She felt touchy suddenly and didn't say anything to Lois.

When her hair was hanging freely, Lois gathered it up in her hands just below her ears. Turning to Angie, she asked again. "Do you think he'd like it this short?"

Trying to laugh off her mood, Angie jokingly said, "It

makes you look like a grasshopper." It did. Lois's face was thinner than Angie's, and the bones in her cheeks stood out more prominently. There was so little roundness in Lois's face that it was almost as if it could hide no secrets. Angie had always felt that she knew what Lois would look like as an old woman. Her face was already hard and almost dried up, the way her bones showed through her skin. And without her braids to frame her face, she looked like a grasshopper to Angie.

"Well, you're no beauty queen yourself, Angie," Lois snapped back. "Just what's so special about you?"

"Is that the only reason you want to cut your hair? So Cultus will notice you? Well, everybody else will notice you then, too," Angie said. The force in her voice surprised her, but it was still there when she continued. "Don't you think you'd look pretty silly dancing in the Longhouse with your hair cut like some white lady ice skater?"

"What are you in such a fit about today? What difference does it make? You're always saying how stupid all that old Indian stuff is anyway. So what if I like Cultus? I'm going to cut my hair so I don't look like an old squaw."

"*Squaw* is a white man's word and it's ugly. It's an insult."

"And just what language are you talking? Since when do you talk Indian language? You're the one who goes 'ugh ugh ugh' when you hear someone talking Indian."

48

"You're the one who does that," Angie insisted.

"You do it too, Angie."

Now that it was out in the open, Angie knew what was making her argue like this with Lois. It was what Marta had told her. Angie felt silly and didn't know what to say to Lois. After a minute or two of silence she said softly, "I think I better go back inside now." She smiled weakly and tried to sound as if nothing had happened. "See you tomorrow, Lois."

Angie got out of the car. This was the first time she and Lois had spoken to each other in anger, and tears were beginning to run down her face. She didn't want Lois to see her crying and know how upset it had made her.

Then when Angie was in front of the car the horn honked. The noise was like being thrown into icy water and Angie couldn't stop the scream that came from her throat.

It was a joke, she thought as soon as she recovered from the shock. It was Lois's way of saying that everything was all right between them. Angie was sure of it, and although she was still trembling she forced another smile at Lois and waved.

Lois didn't return the wave. Angie waited a second longer, and then, badly shaken, she turned to walk back into the Longhouse. But it's okay, she thought. It's okay.

~~~~~

5

When Katla went down to the road with them on Monday morning, Angie told herself she was going to hide behind a tree again. It didn't surprise her; after storming up to McGilvra's door on Saturday, Angie told herself she couldn't be surprised by anything Katla did. She dreaded another scene with the bus driver, that was all, even if she did know Katla would get her way this time. Mr. Johnson would give in and let Cultus ride the bus. Katla would just tell him to do it, and he would. Angie had that much figured out.

But that wasn't the way it turned out at all.

The bus jumped across the creek and backtalked shamefully as it was forced to climb the hill. Everyone but Cultus lined up behind Katla this morning. He leaned up against Angie's tree, but not hiding from the road as she would have done if she were given the chance. Katla had been so sure that Johnson would let him ride the bus that she had made him get dressed and ready for school as usual. They had argued violently, and Angie had been afraid. But Cultus was there, surly and unpredictable, waiting for the bus along with the rest of them.

The bus door was hardly open before Katla spoke. "You take my boy Cultus today, mister bus driver," she stated. Then she stepped closer because Johnson hadn't heard. "You take him today," she said again. "He be good."

The children on the bus stared out the windows at them. There weren't many, just the Winishas and the Mitchells, but Angie felt crawly with their eyes on her.

"No, I can't do that, Mrs. Wallutala," Johnson answered, loudly enough for Cultus to hear where he leaned against the tree. "The only way I can get any support from parents is to kick their kids off when they're bad. If the parents don't like it, they can make their kids behave next time."

"What did he say?" Katla asked in Indian, turning to Angie. She was angry, but Angie couldn't tell whether she wanted a translation or was just startled by Johnson's refusal. Angie was relieved when Katla turned back to the driver and repeated her question, disbelief in her voice.

"You won't take my Cultus?" she said.

"Not until next week, Grandma. I'm sorry." And he was. Angie could tell that by the way he looked at Katla.

"Then you take me?" Katla asked. Angie thought she

51

could hear laughter on the bus. Old fool, she thought to herself bitterly.

"Huh?" the driver asked, this time the disbelief sounding in his voice.

"You take me and I go see them principal, McGilvra."

"Uh, well, okay," he said, but he didn't look very pleased. "What about him?" he asked with a nod in the direction of Cultus. "I still ain't takin' him."

"Cultus," she said, turning to where he glowered, "you go back to the cabin." She spoke to him in Indian in a way that might have fooled Johnson, but it didn't fool any of them. "You stay there, too. If you go near Dan today you'll get whipped," she said threateningly, but evenly, so the threat didn't stick up with any sharp edges in her voice. She warned him about smoking and a few other things that Cultus probably didn't hear. He took off up the road before she was finished—before the bus driver could change his mind. Katla climbed heavily onto the bus and the girls followed her.

"Luke, you get out of that seat and let Mrs. Wallutala sit up front today," Johnson ordered. Luke Winisha looked truly put out by the inconvenience. The seat had his name written above it.

"Well, where am I supposed to sit, then?" he protested without moving. Katla waited.

"Go on," Johnson said. His teeth were clenched.

"All right, all right, I'm goin'." With a mutter Luke went all the way to the last seat, where no one was allowed to sit unless the other seats were full. Johnson didn't say anything to him about it, though, and Katla took Luke's place just behind the driver's seat.

"Angie!" she said, settling herself into the seat like an old hen on a nest.

"Aw, no!" Angie complained. She looked back to the seat that said "Angie-Lois" above it. She had to be back there when Lois got on the bus.

"Come on, you sit with me," Katla said, patting the seat beside her.

"I'm supposed to sit back there, where my name is. The driver makes us sit in the same place every day," she explained desperately. Any change from the ordinary would make it seem as if the quarrel yesterday had built a wall between her and Lois. After what they'd said to each other in the car, Lois might interpret something like this as meaning the end of their friendship. Angie looked to the driver for help.

"It's okay, Angie. You can sit with your grandmother today," Johnson said. Angie could have sworn at him. She sat down next to Katla.

The day was going to be a disaster. She could read it in

the faces of everyone as they got on the bus. First they paused at the top of the steps, gawking at Katla in her traditional tribal dress as if they had never seen anything like it before. Then they would look at Angie with curiosity or disapproval or ridicule before going back to sit down.

Angie understood how they felt. This was their bus, a kids' bus. They didn't want one of the old ones around to mess things up for them, to point out the differences between them and the whites that many of the Indian kids wanted to ignore when they went to the high school in Baker.

Angie's own feelings weren't so clear. Yesterday's secret —don't struggle—was much more difficult to live by once she found herself in the middle of things. When the bus neared Lois's place, Angie thought about getting up and going back to her own seat. What could Katla do? Angie didn't want to disobey, but she had to do something. She was struggling with that choice when she saw Lois.

She'd cut her hair. It wasn't just different. It was terrible, and judging from the defiant scowl on her face, Angie could see that Lois knew it, too. Angie didn't know what to do, so she didn't do anything. She pretended not to see her.

Even though Cultus wasn't there to get them started, the kids were awful the rest of the way to school, far worse than they would have been otherwise. Angie knew what they were thinking: that Johnson would ignore them no matter what they did, since Katla was on the bus. They were right. Angie smelled cigarette smoke, and from the noise level it seemed as if a war was being fought behind her. She didn't turn to look. But when a spitwad, no doubt intended either for Johnson or herself, hit Katla on the cheek with a stinging snap that she could hear, Angie turned to watch Katla.

Tears from the sting of the spitwad were in her eyes, but so was real anger. She turned to face them, and Angie thought she was going to yell at them. She didn't. The kids laughed at her as she looked back at them; confusion, hatred, understanding, and disgust swimming in circles like stranded fish in the drying puddles of her eyes. She turned, then, to look at Johnson, at the back of his head. She didn't say anything to him, either.

Angie felt sorry for her, but she also felt that Katla had it coming. It was like being caught up in a dust devil—the way things were happening—with leaves and dirt spinning around her faster and faster and blinding her until Angie felt she had to strike out at someone or just run away. Then the thought came to her that perhaps this was the way Cultus felt most of the time. She forced herself to calm down.

Angie was glad, for once, when the bus got to school. There was a surge toward the door before it had even opened, and Katla was in front of it. Somehow she managed to get down the steps without falling and was standing in the parking lot, confused, while the kids started into the building.

As soon as Lois was off the bus, Angie caught her by the arm. Lois pulled away without a word, but Angie stuck to her. She would make Lois listen. Then she heard Katla.

"Angie."

Angie's insides crinkled up into a little ball. "I've got to go now," she yelled to her. Lois had gone on without her, and Angie watched her go through the door. "I'll get in trouble if I don't go in," she lied. She had ten minutes before the tardy bell rang.

"I want you to come with me," Katla said to her in Indian. "I don't know where to go."

Angie began to cry. "No," she groaned in despair, and without thinking about it she spoke in Indian. "Why me?" she sputtered. "I didn't do anything, and I sat with you on the bus. Cultus got suspended, not me. Why do I have to go with you?"

"Because I'm a old woman. I can't talk English and I don't know anything. Come on," she said, almost gently. She put out her arm as if to reassure Angie, but Angie didn't let Katla touch her.

"Why can't you leave me alone," she wailed, pulling away from Katla. "You're just ruining everything." Her face was a mess but now she didn't care.

"What kind of talk is that?" Katla scolded. "And what

kind of an Indian are you anyway, Angie, to talk to your Katla like that? You're just as bad as them other kids! Here, blow your nose," she said, handing Angie the handkerchief that she carried tucked into her belt. Then she added, "Nobody said it was easy being an Indian, and this world is no place for a crybaby. Now stop your blubbering and take me to see them McGilvra."

Still crying, Angie led her into the building.

Mrs. Hutchins, the school secretary, asked Angie if something was wrong when she came into the office. Angie looked at the floor and sniffed. "No," she answered. Katla came in the door behind her.

"I wanna talk to them McGilvra," she said. "It's about my boy, Cultus. I'm his grandma."

"Oh yes, Mrs. . . . I'm afraid I can't say your name."

Wallutala, Mildred Wallutala," Katla pronounced it for her.

"Yes, Mrs. . . ." and she gave it an unsuccessful try, laughing at herself good-naturedly. "Mr. McGilvra will be a little late this morning, but he should be here in just a few minutes if you can wait. Won't you have a seat?"

Katla looked disturbed, and Angie expected her to ask why McGilvra was avoiding her the way she had asked his wife on Saturday. Katla was ready to talk, not sit, and Angie knew that this kind of reception only seemed rude to her. Mrs.

Hutchins gestured toward the chairs along the wall and Katla sat down.

She sat rigidly on the edge of the seat. It was the kind with a writing table attached to it, and she looked as if she didn't like being seen sitting in it. Angie knew Katla must be feeling conspicuous and out of place because she felt that way herself. Everyone who came into the office looked at them critically, it seemed—white children with their lunch money, teachers picking up their mail, aides using the machines—all of them seemed to look at them and think, Uh huh, another juvenile delinquent Indian kid and her old grandmother in those funny clothes. And Katla viewed everything with doubt and distrust growing in her eyes. Angie hoped that she would be so put off by it all that she would just get up and leave.

When the tardy bell rang, Mrs. Hutchins asked Angie, "Shouldn't you run along to class?" Katla grunted a nervous, negative response that the secretary understood. Angie had long given up hope of getting out of it by the time McGilvra came in, forty minutes late.

"Good morning," he said to Mrs. Hutchins. He walked on into his office without looking at Katla or Angie. Mrs. Hutchins followed him right in, and Angie could hear her explaining, "Mrs., um, Cultus Wolfe's grandmother has been waiting to see you." She returned immediately to say, "Mr. McGilvra can see you now."

McGilvra sat behind a huge metal desk, as large as the bed she and Carysa shared, Angie thought. Or maybe it just looked big because it was in the middle of the room. It seemed to fill the space like a swimming pool, making them walk around its edges. Angie could see that the top of the desk was made to look like wood. She could see this because there wasn't anything on it.

"Sit down, won't you," McGilvra said pleasantly. Angie sat down. Katla stood.

"I never come here to sit down all morning," she said. "I come here to talk about my boy, Cultus, not sit."

"Yes?" There was an awkward pause.

"Well, he got kicked off them bus," Katla said, unhappy that she had to explain. Didn't he know why Katla was here? Angie wondered.

"Yes," he said again, pleasantly. Too pleasantly.

"Well, I came to talk about it," Katla said impatiently.

"Yes. Well, have a seat, won't you?" McGilvra said again. As soon as Katla was sitting, McGilvra began to talk.

"Now then, Cultus was suspended from the bus by Mr. Johnson because he couldn't obey the rules, wasn't he? I don't remember the specific cause for the suspension, but I understand that the driver warned him about what would happen if he continued to cause a disturbance. When Cultus refused to follow the rules again on Friday, the driver had no choice but to follow through."

During this Katla had looked at Angie as if she needed a translation. Angie felt as if she needed one, too. McGilvra talked like he was some kind of book full of big words, with no glossary in the back. She was happy that Katla spoke for herself.

"I'm a old woman, and maybe I don't understand much what you said. Cultus got kicked off them bus 'cause he a bad boy. I know he sometime a bad boy, but what I'm supposed to do? I ride that bus today. All them kids bad. Indian kids don't act like this when I'm a little girl. Now all them kids bad. What I'm supposed to do with Cultus? That boy too big now for me to whip."

"I don't want you to whip him," McGilvra said, trying to sound shocked. Angie wasn't persuaded. She thought that it was probably exactly what McGilvra wanted. He just didn't want to do it himself.

"No," he went on, "we try to handle these problems in another way."

"Yeah, I see that," Katla said disapprovingly. "You kick 'em out of school. Maybe you don't want 'em here."

"All we want is for parents to know what their children

60

do on the bus. When they get in trouble, the parents should take care of it, not the driver. Or the principal. And Cultus wasn't suspended from school. His behavior here is probably no better than it is on the bus, but he is expected to be here every day this week all the same. Did he come in this morning?"

"How he's supposed to do that? Look here, Mr. Principal, I know Cultus a bad boy. I know that already. Nobody don't have to kick him off them bus for me to know that. Why he's bad? Know what I think? I think he don't like school. And then you tells him, 'Cultus, you behave or we goin' kick you off them bus so's you can't ride it to school no more.' What you do then, mister, if you hates school like him?"

"I don't have any quick answers for why children his age don't like school. Boys seem to have more trouble than girls, and it seems especially hard for Indian boys. Maybe part of it is the long ride into town, but there's nothing we can do about that. Other reservations still have boarding schools. Even then, we'd still have to bus some into Baker because of the segregation laws."

Angie didn't know what segregation laws were, so she was sure Katla didn't know either. But Katla did know what a boarding school was, and she said, "We don't want no more boarding school."

"Anyway, I'm sure that part of the reason Indian children

don't like this school is that long trip on the bus," he went on. "And I know how easy it is for kids to get in trouble when they have to ride too far."

"Somebody gots to make them kids behave," Katla insisted, although McGilvra looked as if he'd listened to all he was going to. "It don't do no good to kick 'em off them bus. That way you giving 'em how they want it."

McGilvra looked bored now, as if he'd heard it all before a thousand times, but he answered Katla. "There's everyone's safety to be considered, too," he reasoned, the boredom in his voice making Angie squirm to get out of there. "What if one of these pranks of Cultus's caused the driver to go off the road with a busload of children?"

"That's what I been saying." Katla's voice was full of frustration. "Somebody got to make them kids behave." Katla was getting loud, and Angie considered nudging her with her elbow. She wasn't really shouting. It was more like McGilvra was on the other side of a bigger room. Whenever Katla spoke to him, he didn't seem to hear, so she had raised her voice a little. "The schools or them driver got to make them kids be good, or like you says they gonna cause a wreck or something. I was on that bus this morning, and them kids was *bad*."

"The bus driver can't be a parent to a busload of children," McGilvra said with conviction. A lot of the pleasantness had gone out of his voice, and Angie knew it was time for them to leave. She sat on the edge of her chair, hoping Katla would take the hint. "And parents can't always expect teachers and bus drivers to raise their children for them."

That made Katla mad. "So what I'm supposed to do with Cultus? I can't make him be good on them bus, and I ain't gonna let him quit school neither. You tell me what I'm gonna do."

McGilvra grunted sympathetically and shrugged. "Well," he said at last, "having talked with you, I don't see any reason Cultus can't ride the bus to school in the morning. He'll have to obey the rules, of course," he cautioned. "I'll talk with the driver about it."

"And what if he don't obey the rules?" Katla asked forcefully. After a short, thoughtful pause the telephone rang with near perfect timing, and McGilvra never got around to answering Katla's question.

~~~~~

6

This place stinks," Katla said. The two of them stood outside the office. After waiting for McGilvra to finish his telephone conversation—a long one—he had turned to ask them, "Is that all?" So that had been all. He was dialing the phone as they left the office, and it had been Mrs. Hutchins who spoke to them. "Have a nice day, now," she had said.

"This place stinks," Katla repeated, wadding all her wrinkles up around her nose to make the right face.

"Huh?" Angie asked, sniffing. It smelled all right to her. "What do ya mean 'stinks'?" she asked.

"Well, smell it." Angie did. There were just the usual school smells. Paper, floor wax, disinfectant, and people. Angie thought she must be used to it. "No Indian smells," Katla explained. "Smells like a school." Angie asked herself in exasperation what else it should smell like, but thinking of Indian smells, and home, brought a more important question to mind.

"How're you going to get home?" she asked. Too late, it occurred to Angie that the only way home was the way they'd come. And that meant that Katla had the whole day on her hands with no place to go and nothing to do. "I gotta go now, Katla," she said, but escape looked hopeless. "I'm supposed to be in Health now. I already missed P.E., and Miss Matson is gonna think I skipped."

"Where are you going now?" Katla asked. She looked down the hall and back at Angie.

"To Health, I said. I gotta go to school, ya know," Angie answered. But she knew she didn't stand a chance. Katla seemed to think a moment, her eyes moving with uncertainty over her surroundings. Her face, which was as permanent as stone and as changeable as clay all at the same time, right now looked childish to Angie. She was a little girl on her first day of school, waiting to be told where to go.

"I want to see this Health," she said with decision. Off they went, Angie leading.

Katla stopped her outside the door when they got to room six. The hall was deserted. Angie was nervous about walking in late; it was going to be pure torture doing what Katla told her. She didn't argue, though. She didn't want Katla to yell at her now. Angie opened the door and, leaving it open, went into the room and up to Miss Matson.

"Where have you been, Angie? You're late," Miss Matson said to her, but she softened when Angie got close enough that she could see she'd been crying. That's why she was Angie's and Lois's favorite teacher. She really made you work hard, but you didn't mind because she was so nice. "Is something the matter, sweetheart?" she asked. That was another reason the girls liked her. They were supposed to be too old for that kind of thing, but Miss Matson still called them "sweetheart."

"My grandma's here today," she whispered, so softly that Miss Matson bent closer and asked her to repeat what she'd said.

"Oh. Is that why you're late? Sit down, please."

"She's right outside the door, I mean," Angie blurted out. Behind her she heard Lois snicker, and the blood rushed to her face. "She told me to ask you if it's okay for her to come in." She whispered again.

"Oh, well now. Does she need to talk with me? Ask her to come in, please." Now Miss Matson looked nervous, too.

"No, she just wants to watch is all. She's spending the whole day with me."

Miss Matson went to the door herself and asked Katla to come in. Katla looked as if she were going to be hanged and Miss Matson were the hangman. Her moccasins scraped the floor, making a lisping sound as she dragged her feet. When she sat down next to Angie her beads rattled on the desk top.

"Now let's please open our books to page one hundred twelve," the teacher said from the front of the room once she had Katla installed. And they read about poise. Angie tried to pay attention, but she just couldn't. Not with Lois in the room. She was sure that the things Lois whispered to Elsie Mitchell were about her and Katla. Lois kept looking their way with a snide little smirk, but Elsie looked as if Lois made her uncomfortable. Finally Miss Matson asked her to stop whispering.

There was another rattle of beads on her desk top as Katla turned to look back at Lois. Then she turned to Angie and said, "What happened to Lois's hair? She have lice?"

She said it in Indian, but the word *Lois* stood out so that everyone knew who Katla was talking about. The Indian girls, of course, knew what she had said, Lois included. This was the first time she had mentioned Lois's haircut, and Angie knew it wasn't a real question. Katla was expressing her disapproval of Lois. Some Indian girls cut their hair, but not the ones who were active in the Longhouse. Katla had nothing but scorn for those girls, and now Lois was one of them.

"Ugh, ugh, ugh," they heard Lois mutter. Miss Matson clearly didn't know what was happening, but she stopped it.

"Lois, I'm sending you to the office. I want you to be there after class, and we'll talk this over with the principal."

The class returned to their books. As near as Angie could figure out by the end of the period, "poise" was something Miss Matson had but the rest of them didn't, especially her and Katla.

The day dragged on. There was one more class, lunch, then three more classes in the afternoon, and the only time Katla left Angie was when Miss Matson invited her into the teachers' room to eat. Katla clearly didn't want to go without Angie, but she did. Angie stayed in the cafeteria and looked for Lois.

"She's supposed to stay in study hall all day," Elsie told her. "Them McGilvra don't want her to do anything else today because your Katla's here. Lois is crazy mad. Mostly I think because of her hair. What did she go and do that for anyway? It's ugly! What your Katla said about it was sure funny," she finished, laughing.

Angie didn't know what to say, so she said, "I think it looks nice."

"Liar," Elsie said.

When Katla came back into the cafeteria, Angie was afraid to ask what Miss Matson had said. It was Katla who talked about it first, but only at the end of the day.

"Lois always like that?" she asked Angie. "Them lady teacher asked me about her."

Angie was getting ready to go out to the bus, rattling

around in the locker she shared with Lois. Lois liked clutter, and the locker held her collection. Angie, by moving fast, and with a little luck, was able to shut the door without upsetting everything onto the floor.

"Like what? What did you tell Miss Matson?" Angie responded after slamming the door.

"Like she got no sense, and proud of it. That's what I told her, too, that teacher." Angie wondered if Katla was speaking English because of the "ugh ugh, ugh" business.

"She's my friend, Katla." Angie's face almost let go, but she held herself back and didn't cry.

Katla grunted. "She should act like a friend, then," she said.

Lois was already outside. She was standing more or less in line behind Linda Schultz when Linda left the line to flirt with a group of boys at the bicycle racks. Before Linda walked away, she put her books at Lois's feet and announced to her that she got "place-backs." Lois made a face, but didn't say anything that Angie could hear.

She watched Lois with interest. Linda was white, and Angie knew Lois well enough to be sure she wouldn't let a chance like this go by. She had picked up the large green book from the top of the stack at her feet and was writing something in it. Katla was watching too.

"Lois!" she said loud enough to stop all the chatter. Every

frog in the pond was silent so suddenly that Angie knew something awful was about to happen. Alert, she watched Katla, as did everyone.

"What?" Lois replied testily. Sure, she had written a bad word, but not the worst one she could think of.

"What you writin' in them white girl's book?" Katla demanded. Linda came back from the bicycle racks but had enough sense to stay out of the way. Lois merely closed the book and held it behind her without looking up or answering.

"Give me that book," Katla ordered. A tremor ran through Katla's voice, powerfully, like the ground shaking when a truck goes by. Lois threw the book on the ground and started to walk away. Angie could see she was scared, but she walked away arrogantly so no one would notice how scared. Katla had taken all the disrespect she could for one day. Lois had just started to run when Katla grabbed her roughly by the arm.

"Ow-uch! Let go you old witch!" she cried out. Then she swore at Katla in front of everyone. The children watched in horror as Katla slapped Lois, and Lois struck back. Wildly, she hit Katla with both hands, pushing, and Katla fell to the ground. Still stuck in their tracks, the children watched as Lois ran blindly away. No one ran after her.

When Katla groaned, Angie seemed to return to life. Linda Schultz was there first, trying to lift Katla into a sitting position. "Leave her alone," Angie screamed at her, and at the rest of the children. "What are you looking at? Get out of here. Go on and leave us alone," she sobbed, panicked.

"Are you all right, Katla?" she asked. Katla sat up holding her wrist. Her old face was smoothed out in shock and she didn't answer. The kids crowded closer and Angie shouted for them to move back.

It was Linda who came from the building leading Mr. McGilvra. She was so excited she was running in circles in front of him, but he didn't seem to be in any big hurry. He was carrying his suit jacket over his arm, as if he knew he was going to be out of his office for a while.

"Have you had an accident?" he asked soothingly, standing over them. Angie answered when Katla sat silent. The wrinkles were returning to her face.

"I think she broke her arm, Mr. McGilvra," Angie said. "Can you take us to the hospital?" As he left them to get his car, Angie heard Katla swear at him under her breath. She was going to be all right.

———

7

I t's like when you try to break a green stick," the doctor said. "The stick doesn't break in half, it just splits where it bends. That's why they call it a green-stick fracture." He was a small, young man with a striking, bushy beard down to his shirt collar. He stood over Katla, speaking to her warmly, but she wouldn't look at him. She was ruffled about something. She was looking at nothing in particular, but she was staring at that nothing so hard she was almost cross-eyed. She didn't seem to care what kind of fracture it was.

Angie, unlike her grandmother, couldn't take her eyes off the young doctor. Maybe it was just that he was such a small man that the beard looked that much bigger; it sure was a big beard, though. Not like anything an Indian man could grow. And sensing that she was the only one listening to him, he turned toward Angie.

"Really remarkable for a person your grandmother's age," he said. "Normally a person's bones get more brittle as they get older. She's lucky to have such healthy bones. It won't take so long for it to heal." He ran his hand self-consciously over his beard, perhaps because Angie was watching it so closely. Then he looked at his wrist watch. "Well, she'll be in here a couple of days before I put her arm in a cast, just in case there are any complications. I'll look in on you in the morning," he finished, and left the room.

Katla lay in bed with her arm propped between sandbags. But she didn't look weak, or hurt, or any of the things Angie imagined an old woman with a broken arm ought to look. She looked mad enough to tear the room apart. Angie figured that it must be about something the doctor had done to her.

And just then one of the other three women in the room got out of her bed and walked past Angie to the bathroom. Looking at the lady from behind, Angie giggled. The gown she wore was open at the back and the lady's indignity was showing.

"What you laughing at?" Katla snarled. So that was it. Angie couldn't help herself. She tried, but she burst out laughing at Katla now. "You stop that or I'm gonna get out of this bed and pop you one." A second later she added, "Well, everybody has to wear one of those." Then she laughed too. A deep, single cackle that must have hurt her arm because she groaned and laughed more softly. "You should have seen me, trying to keep my back to the wall while they were taking pictures of my arm," she said. And it was funny, but for some reason Angie began to cry.

"You are such a crybaby, Angie!" Katla had scolded her with those very same words that morning when they went into the school office. This time she said it so tenderly that Angie only cried harder.

After a short silence Katla asked, just as tenderly, "Why did she do this?" It was a real question, but Angie didn't have the words to tell Katla. The answer was there like an itch she couldn't scratch. "Was it because I grabbed her in front of everyone?" Katla asked.

That was part of it, but Angie knew that wasn't the only reason. "No," she answered. She looked up as she said it. She met Katla's eyes, clear and intelligent, going over her with sharp inquiry. She knew she was coming up short in Katla's measurements; she wanted to explain, but she just couldn't.

"Maybe I'm just too old," Katla said. "I can't understand kids anymore." That was all she said, and Angie didn't disagree.

Katla was watching television when Dan came in. She was the only one watching it. The other women in the room had visitors, and the set was on a shelf above Angie's head. Angie didn't move the chair, so she only listened.

She listened well enough to know that Katla switched the

channels about every four or five minutes, probably not so much bored by the programs as interested in playing with the remote-control dial. The nurse had shown her how to use it after she had pushed the buzzer on her pillow half a dozen times to call her in for nothing. After the nurse showed her how to turn on the TV, Katla didn't call her again.

She didn't turn it off when Dan came in. "Who did this?" he asked, standing at the end of her bed with his feet spread and his hands on his hips. Then he answered his own question. "Lois?" he said.

Katla's eyes didn't leave the television screen as she said, "Took you long enough to get here. Who told you?"

"Them bus driver, Johnson. He went to the police station and they called me up on the radio in my truck." Cultus and Marta came into the room carrying Cokes. "I was clear up the river checking fish traps and it took me a long time to get here."

"Uh huh," Katla said. "Sure you was. They keep beer in them fish traps, do they?" Everyone laughed but Dan. He started to say something else, but Katla cut him short. "Where's Carysa?" she asked, finally turning away from her television program to look at him. "You didn't leave her home all alone, did you?"

"She's here," Dan answered, but shaking his head as if he

didn't believe himself. He put his hands in his pockets and looked for something to lean against. Two minutes before, he had marched in as if he were going to pull the world around by its ear, and already Katla had him so confused he didn't know whether he was coming or going. Hospital gown or not, Angie thought, Katla still wears the pants in this family.

"She's out front, I mean. Where the office is," Dan explained. She can't come in because you're supposed to be twelve. Why did she do it?"

"Lois? I guess because I grabbed her by the arm," Katla answered. There was irony in her voice and she looked at Angie tellingly as she said it.

"Well, maybe you better tell us about it," Cultus inserted, sounding tough and taking a swig from his Coke bottle in a swashbuckling way. This was the last time his interest in the conversation surfaced before drowning in the TV. Katla told Dan about it.

"I caught her writing something nasty in some white girl's book," she said. "Then when she tried to run away I grabbed her by the arm. I didn't mean to hurt her. All I wanted to do was talk to her. About what a little fool she was. All the Indian kids acted like they were stupid or something. Maybe their teachers don't know any better, but I do.

"Maybe I can't talk English, but I'm not blind. So I was

76

trying to talk to Lois, to tell her what a little fool she was. And then she pushed me." She was making herself sound more innocent than she was, Angie thought. She had slapped Lois, too.

"She just pushed you for no reason, then," Dan concluded. Katla looked blankly back at the television set, neither agreeing nor disagreeing. Dan had a determined look on his face.

Angie felt that this was the time to say something to defend her friend, but she still couldn't find the right words. To say, "She was afraid," or "It was an accident," would only turn Dan and Cultus against her. So Angie didn't say anything.

By the time the nurse came into the room to announce that visiting hours were over, all five of them were absorbed in the TV. Katla continued to play with the remote control, to their annoyance, but she was the sick one so they indulged her without complaints. They left Katla shuffling channels and were ambushed in the lobby by Carysa, who was waiting for them like a snake under a rock. She accused them of forgetting about her, which was true no matter how much they denied it.

"They don't let shrimps inside a hospital," Angie told her. Carysa was a spicy little shrimp without Katla around, as Marta and Angie were about to find out.

The whole household seemed to fall apart with Katla gone,

and the next morning was a bad one for Angie. She and Marta tried to get Carysa up on time, fed, and dressed, but with both of them grouchy from too little sleep and each fighting to have her own way, they had a rough time of it. And they never should have waked Cultus.

First it was Carysa. When she refused to go to the pump to wash, Marta blew up at her. "You do what you're told," she scolded, giving the little girl a good shake. Angie would rather touch bugs than have that cold water touch her, so she was on Carysa's side in this argument even if she didn't say anything right away.

"You're not the boss around here," Carysa answered Marta, and then swore in her meaningless way, saying the words she connected with anger from having heard Cultus during his fits. The outburst woke Cultus.

"Can't you both shut up so I can sleep?" he shouted, pulling the blankets up over his head.

"Couldn't we heat the water on the stove?" Angie suggested after a while, and softly so as not to rouse Cultus again. Angie thought he was only pretending to sleep, but they would let him stay in bed as long as possible this morning. It was easier getting ready without having him throw tantrums about everything, and he could get himself ready just before the bus came.

But Marta insisted, since Katla always had, that the cold

water was good for them. "It's the Indian way," she pronounced, with the result that only Marta washed that morning.

And breakfast was hardly more successful. Angie burned her fingers whenever she tried to drop the batter into the hot fat the way Katla did. Carysa claimed the bread was doughy in the middle, which it was, and Angie had no more than fed her little sister when they heard the bus honk its horn down at the road.

"Carysa!" Marta ordered. "You get your coat on and then run and tell them driver to wait. Cultus! It's time you got up. You know them Johnson won't wait more'n four or five minutes."

"I don't have to go to school," Cultus shouted, sitting on the edge of his bed. "What did you have to wake me up for?" He put on his pants, so Angie figured he was getting ready in spite of what he said. She should have kept quiet.

"I was there!" she argued from across the room. "Them McGilvra said you was supposed to go to school the rest of the week, and he was going to fix it up with the driver."

"You shut up!" he growled, and he was up and at her before she could run.

She heard Marta say, "Cultus, don't! I'll tell Katla!"

"I'll teach you," he said. He hit her in the upper arm and Angie felt the knuckles go all the way to the bone. He could have broken it if he'd wanted to. "Don't you ever tell me what to do."

For good measure Cultus slugged her again in the same place, but not as hard. Then he walked out of the cabin in his bare feet and they heard the outhouse door slam. Marta picked up her coat and Angie's and they both left quickly.

Down the road Marta asked, "You okay, *inima leah?*"

The tender words, "my little sister," helped, and Angie sniveled, "Yes." Marta helped her put on her coat. "Only I don't want to come back here until Katla comes home."

When Johnson saw Angie he asked what happened. "She bumped her arm," Marta answered for her. "And Cultus ain't comin', so you don't need to wait."

The bus crawled up the hill like a half-squashed bug. As it reached the top of the mesa, it picked up speed and rolled along through the familiar scenery. Broken and beautiful, the high desert plateau plunged from rimrock into deep ravines, only to appear on the same level miles away like a piece of the same jigsaw puzzle.

However hard she looked out the window, though, Angie couldn't see anything but the look on Cultus's face just before he hit her.

Soon the bus wound down the other side of the mesa and stopped at Lois's. Angie's mind raced as Lois stepped through the fence and turned to help Willie. What could she say? At least she would have a chance to say *something,* and Lois would have to listen. Angie's eyes shot up to the "Angie-Lois" sign above her, and then to Lois, who had stopped to talk to the driver.

Angie sat up, ready for the earth to move when Lois sat down next to her with her usual disregard for her spine. But Lois walked right on past, all the way to the back of the bus, without looking to either side as if everyone were invisible. Angie felt eyes boring into the back of her neck all the way to school. So that's how it's going to be, Angie said to herself.

⌒⌒⌒⌒⌒

And then, just when she had decided that the easiest thing was to hate Lois for hating her, Angie found herself jumping to protect her. It was at lunch. She sat with Dorothy Winisha and Elsie Mitchell, but because Lois was in the cafeteria Angie felt the same hot discomfort on her neck, as if she were still riding the bus with Lois watching her from behind. It was as if something were crawling out from under her collar; she couldn't help raising a hand to the spot.

"I think it's just awful what them Lois done to your grandma," Dorothy said. She didn't let the conversation interrupt her chewing. "I just can't believe she'd do that."

"She didn't mean to do it," Angie found herself saying.

"Well it didn't look like no accident to me," Elsie joined in. "And now look at the way she's acting. Somebody should teach her a lesson."

"Don't worry," Dorothy vowed, "she'll get what's coming to her. I'll bet Cultus will see to that. Just like he seen to that Loomis with a can opener." And both girls laughed.

"There's nothing coming to her," Angie insisted. "And Cultus better leave her alone, too." She couldn't stand the thought of Cultus hurting Lois.

"Then why's she acting like there was? Sure looks like it wasn't no accident."

"I don't know. Oh, it's all mixed up. If only Katla would mind her own business," Angie said. And she thought to herself, if only I could explain it to Lois. I could explain it to her so she'd understand, but not Dorothy and Elsie.

Angie thought up until the end of school that she'd get her chance to explain. Lois was shifty, but she couldn't avoid Angie all day; sooner or later they would have to meet at their locker. They had too much traffic in and out of it between classes not to meet there sometime during school.

So it was like discovering a burglary when she noticed, just before bus time, that Lois's things were missing. At first she couldn't tell what was wrong, and she didn't figure it out until she started to close the door. It was too easy. And then she saw that all Lois had left were squashed, sticky paper cups, some candy wrappers, and a very black banana peel. For the second time that day she said to herself, so that's how it's going to be.

Angie wasn't able to untangle her emotions. She had knots at both ends, at home and at school, and there wasn't anyplace for her in between. Cultus gave her a stare that night that said he was sorry, but it still held the threat of more if she didn't watch her step. Angie spent the evening outside, until she was sure he'd gone to bed, and then Katla came home the next day.

It hadn't been so long, only two days without her, but as the girls walked up to the cabin Wednesday evening after school, her voice was a cheerful sound. In a way, that is. It probably wasn't sounding as cheerful to Dan and Cultus.

"You, Dan," Katla spat out. "Too busy to come up and check on these kids. Now look at this place. Angie's too lazy to carry wood to the smokehouse. Marta's too lazy to wash dishes, and Carysa won't pick up her clothes. And Cultus is too lazy even to get out of bed. He's like a big lazy dog. He ought to be kicked. And Powwow is only two days away. How am I supposed to get the Longhouse ready and cook for the dancers when I can't even come home from the hospital and find the dishes washed and the beds made?"

It was good to have her back.

When the girls walked in, she turned on them. "Put your

83

things away and help me clean up this mess," she said. Angie and Marta exchanged a look that held amusement and relief. Katla would have to take it easy for a while. She couldn't do the housework herself, but having her back was enough to put the household in order again. Angie and Marta got right to work, and happily.

But not Carysa. She had found her independence in the past two days, and she wasn't about to give it up so easily.

"Carysa, clean up those clothes and then go get water so the girls can wash the dishes," Katla ordered with a scowl. Carysa threw her coat on the floor and started for the door, but not with the bucket.

Katla had a cast on one arm, but broken arm or not she was capable of dealing with a seven-year-old who wouldn't mind. "After what I just said, why did she do that?" she seemed to ask everyone in the room. "Now pick it up!" Carysa stopped before going through the door. "Pick it up, I said." And Carysa did it. That was the end of the rebellion.

"She's been sassy the whole time you've been gone," Marta said, evidently not satisfied when Katla didn't do more to the little imp. "And Cultus . . ."

"You mind your own business and get to work," Katla answered sharply. "You got a lot to do. Powwow is only two days away."

8

〰〰〰〰〰〰〰〰〰〰〰〰〰〰〰〰〰〰〰〰〰〰〰

Y ou should have let Katla show you how," Marta said. Angie grumped out a wordless response. "Well, you should have," Marta insisted. "She tried to show you how to do beadwork just last week and you didn't want to listen. Now look at . . ."

"Okay, okay, okay," Angie cut her off. People were always saying I told you so. Angie hated it, especially from Marta.

They sat on opposite sides of the table, still cluttered with the morning dishes, working on their leggin's. These were the new ones Katla had promised them, but she didn't get around to the beadwork. Now that she was unable to do it, because of her arm, the girls were trying to put the beads on themselves. The beads were spread out between them on one of Katla's large scarfs.

It was quiet work. It took all of Angie's concentration to string the beads onto her needle and thread; then pushing the needle through the leather as she tacked down the string of beads was painstaking and prickly work. The needle seemed always to come through the leather a quarter of an inch away from the beads to be tacked down, and right under a finger. Angie's hands were moist with tension, and that only made handling the needle more difficult.

"At least she let us stay home to get this done," Angie said during a pause in her work. She found that she had to look at objects across the room every now and then for her eyes to focus.

"But two days isn't enough to get it all done," Marta said, squinting over her beads. " 'Specially since we have to do everything else, too. It would have been a lot easier if she would have sent Carysa to school and let us stay home alone."

Angie responded with a wistful sigh. It was a strangely dishonest feeling, staying home when she wasn't sick, and the sound of the bus, its horn honking like a distressed goose, nagged at Angie as she remembered it. Not that she had been all that eager to go to school. School was a drag, but not quite as bad as staying home on a rainy day. Outside rain fell from the eaves with the kind of slurps a dog makes as it laps up water from a dish. And thinking this, she stuck the needle into her finger deep enough to make it bleed.

"Aw, nuts!" She threw the leggin' down in a heap on the messy table. Marta didn't say anything, but she gave Angie a look that plainly said, I told you so. Angie was on the verge of an argument with Marta when she heard a stir in

Katla's bedroom. She picked up the leggin', sprinkling beads on the floor as she did it, and tried to look hard at work when Katla shuffled into the room.

"What's the matter now, Angie?" she asked wearily. "Let me see." Katla took the leggin' from Angie and held it in her good hand as she examined the beads. She wasn't impressed.

"You got too many beads in this row," she said, pointing to the place with the swollen fingers that stuck out of her cast. The fingers looked like—what?—Angie couldn't say for sure. But they looked like something it wasn't proper to look at too directly or too long.

"And you didn't tack them down every three beads like I told you. These will flop around when you dance in them." She handed the leggin' back to Angie. The eagle Katla had traced on it for her was barely started; she had done four rows on one wing. That had taken her nearly an hour. The whole pattern was only about six inches square, but there were two of them, one eagle for each leggin'. Angie was so frustrated she felt she was about to burst into flames, but not because she wanted to quit. She wanted her beadwork to look as nice as Katla's always did.

"This is how it should look," Katla said, holding Marta's under her nose for inspection. Marta had one whole wing almost finished. The rows were straight and tacked down tightly.

It was this sort of thing that made Angie think unkindly of Marta. She could never do anything as well as Marta. "How did you do that so fast?" she asked irritably.

"It's not so hard once you get the hang of it. It just takes practice. You should have . . ."

Angie would have flared up at Marta, but Katla didn't give her a chance. "Here," she instructed, handing the scissors to Angie. Katla was right-handed, and she had broken her left arm. Still, everything she did looked awkward. She stood sideways so much of the time, protecting her arm, and even seemed to walk that way. It was as if half of her had been surgically removed. "Cut them out," she said. "You should be finishing your dress, anyway. You can bead your leggin's some other time."

Cutting out her work, Angie thought she might never learn to bead. In another part of her thoughts, she told herself she didn't care.

Katla told her how to put the fringe on her skin dress before saying, "I got to go lay down again. I don't feel so good." The fringe was simple. She cut strips of leather and put them through holes along the shoulders, hips, sleeves, and hem of the dress. There were lots of them to be put on, but it wasn't hard to do. She was almost finished when she had to stop to fix lunch. She might have finished it that afternoon if Dan hadn't come to the cabin just as they were eating.

"If you came to take us to the Longhouse, you made sure you came early enough for lunch," Katla said by way of greeting him.

Dan, dripping from the downpour outside, laughed off the accusation. "Come here and see what I got," he said, so mysteriously that everyone followed him out into the rain. He had put the aluminum canopy on the back of the pickup because of the weather, and beneath it lay two deer, both does, gutted. "That ought to feed them drummers for a while," he said proudly.

The girls were disappointed. It only meant more messy work for them, but it was Carysa who said, "Is that all? You mean we came out here and got all wet just to look at two dead deer?" Angie wondered what she was expecting, a bicycle? Carysa wouldn't even have to prepare the meat.

Cultus was the only one of them really excited, asking all sorts of questions so Dan would tell him about the hunt. Where, he wanted to know, and how many shots had it taken with that new scope, and did he have to carry them far? Cultus had long wished that Dan could take him hunting some Saturday instead of having to drive them all to Red Salmon. Once Dan let Cultus shoot the big rifle out in back of the smokehouse, but he had never been hunting except for varmints with Katla's old single-shot .22.

Katla said, "Thanks, Dan," but then added, "now we know what you do when you're supposed to be putting out forest fires."

But Katla wasn't about to puncture the balloon of his pride with her sarcastic darts. "Now what kind of forest fires am I going to put out on a day like this?" he asked.

They bundled up after lunch and rode to the Longhouse. The rain pounding on the canopy and the stare of the two animals in the back of the pickup with them gave the children a gloomy frame of mind that stuck with Angie the rest of the day. The building was cold and empty. She had on her school shoes, not moccasins, and her footsteps rang out clearly in the room. Angie knew she should be feeling closer to her family, to her people. That was what Powwow was for. But she couldn't shake the mood she was in; everything seemed to be falling farther and farther apart.

She tried to imagine what the room would be like in two days, with feathered dancers wearing bells on their leggin's and people crowded along the edge and back of the room to watch them perform. She would dance, hot and nervous, yet hypnotized by the piercing chant and the urgent throb of the big war drum. It didn't help. Beneath it all, Angie brooded about Lois.

She started working in the kitchen. Angie and Marta were led directly to the messy jobs by Katla, who didn't "feel so good" and who, of course, couldn't do kitchen work with her arm in a plaster cast. "It might melt," she said. Angie couldn't help thinking that she would rather be in school.

Angie only planned to help Marta with the meat until she could get out of it without causing trouble for herself. Under Katla's direction, they quartered one of the deer and then began cutting up one of the quarters. The meat would be cooked in the traditional way, by boiling it in water, so it had to be cut into stew-sized pieces. Angie disliked this job, not because she was squeamish but because it took so long. It was hard work, and the two of them had nearly finished it before Angie was able to manage an escape.

She was rescued by Ellen Jim and Mildred Wenna, two old women roughly Katla's age, who came into the kitchen with a burlap bag of roots each. "You haven't been digging today, have you?" Katla said to them in Indian.

"No," they laughed. Angie always thought it strange that Katla and her friends could laugh so easily over nothing. "We dug them yesterday, before it started to rain," Ellen explained. The three of them included Marta in their conversation as if she were already one of them. That was Marta. And except for differences caused by their ages, differences which didn't seem all that great as Angie looked at them now, Marta might easily have been one of them. At sixteen she was bigger than they were, with the same full figure but not, of course, as bent and settled into the solidly squat shape of the older women. Most of the difference was in her face. This too was fuller, and where the older women had wrinkles, Marta had acne. But it wasn't bad acne. Marta was a truly beautiful girl able to flash a smile of even, white teeth. While the old women weren't exactly beautiful in the same way, and their grins revealed lonely stumps of teeth gnarled on the bare ridges of their gums, it didn't take much imagination to see them in Marta's face as they might have looked sixty years younger. Talking Indian with ease, she just seemed to belong to the group.

But not Angie. She was sent to the sink to clean the roots. Since it was still early in the spring, most of the roots were two types, *luksh* and *piakhe,* with a few *haush* mixed in. They had to be peeled first, then washed. The *luksh* was round, good to eat fresh from the earth, but it was used more often either boiled or ground up to make dumplings or flat cakes. *Piakhe* looked like a tree root, bent, branched, and hairy with rootlets, only smaller. It tasted bitter and a little like kerosene to Angie. Both of these were regular items at Katla's table.

Angie slipped the skins off the roots skillfully, easily, and then rinsed them in warm water. She knew they were supposed to be washed in cold water like all vegetables, but she didn't understand the reason for it when they were just going to be boiled in a day or two anyway. At first the warm water felt so good that she didn't mind the job at all. She popped an occasional *luksh* into her mouth and listened to the talk at her back. After a short while two sacks full of roots began to look like a lot of roots. She jumped at the chance to get out of the kitchen when she heard Dan shouting from the other end of the Longhouse.

"Hey Cultus, somebody, come here and help me for a minute."

Cultus didn't move from the couch near the kitchen door. As soon as he saw that he wasn't needed—Angie hurried past him saying "I'll go"—he returned to his comic books.

Dan was on a stepladder, trying to hang crepe paper. Carysa had dropped her broom in the middle of the floor and was trying to roll up a strip of paper he'd dropped. Dan was rolling the strip from his end and telling Carysa to leave it alone.

"Angie, will you take that from her before she wrecks it? Carysa, let Angie have it, will you? And you can stay out here and help me. This takes four hands and I ain't no octopus."

"An octopus got eight hands, isn't it, Angie?" she piped up. She handed the wrinkled paper strip to Angie and went back to her broom when Dan ordered her to finish sweeping the floor. Marta stayed in the kitchen like the good girl she was, but Angie preferred a little guilt to a lot of work; she managed to spend the rest of the afternoon puttering with the decorations. And the Longhouse looked a little brighter to her by the end of the day.

The crepe paper lightened Angie's spirits, but the real Powwow decorations would be the dancers in their costumes. She reflected glumly upon her own, made up of leftovers from last year and an unfinished dress. She knew she couldn't win. But that wasn't what troubled Angie. This was the year she and Lois had planned to have buffalo dresses together. She wondered if the Powwow was going to be anything but more hard work for her now.

The next day the Buffalo Lodge Drummers, from Crow, Montana, were due to arrive. Friday, for the most part, was spent getting ready for them. They would be received royally, since the Buffalo Lodge Drummers were recording stars. Stacey's store in Red Salmon sold their records, and Marta had bought one even though they had no record player at home. She could only listen to it at Dan's place.

The drummers would be paid from the money the Powwow Committee had raised by selling beadwork, but that wouldn't be all they would receive from their friends at the Badger Creek Longhouse. The give-away was traditional among Katla's people, and it would be an important part of the Powwow. The people of the Badger Creek Longhouse would want to impress the drummers with their generosity and wealth by giving them blankets and beadwork, among other things.

Katla liked to give blankets. That meant a shopping trip to Red Salmon was necessary. Then there was the laundry to do, and showers were overdue, too.

That Friday the children got two dimes for hot water, since they also had two weeks' worth of dirt to wash off. Angie luxuriated in the steamy little room until she thought her whole body might pucker up like her fingertips. Then she folded laundry for Katla.

Lunch was late, and a disappointment. Laundry day usually meant treats, and sometimes a hamburger at the drive-in. Today Katla was so anxious to be back in time to greet the drummers that they didn't even stop at home. They drove straight to the Longhouse, and Marta fixed a late lunch for them of canned soup and fried bread.

After that, Angie was free to work on her dress. She shared the lumpy couch with Cultus, who was rereading the stack of battered, incomplete comics for the millionth time. Except for when Dan made them move the couch so he could put up the bleachers by the kitchen, Angie was undisturbed, and she finished the fringe. Her dress wasn't very fancy. It didn't have beads or shells on it. But it was finished in time for the Powwow.

The arrival of the drummers, near evening, was accompanied by all the commotion that surrounds celebrities. They drove a mobile home brightly painted with Indian designs. The sign on the side announced the Buffalo Lodge Drummers in large red letters painted to look as if they were made from arrows.

Almost ignoring the people who had waited all day for them, the drummers set themselves up immediately. Two of them carried in the large war drum between them. Arranging their chairs in a circle around it, they began to tap the drum with their beaters, as if trying it out to make sure it still sounded the same. Then they sang a greeting song to the people in the Longhouse. Then they sang another, and it began to look and sound like Powwow. Dan fiddled with the audio system until the loudspeakers on the roof of the building filled the empty hills with music, and as that drew people in, the Longhouse began to look busy. Some of the cooks began taping the music on small cassette recorders, and some of the younger people began a round dance.

Angie couldn't dance with them because she didn't have her moccasins, but her school shoes tapped the floor to the beat of the drum as she sat watching from the couch. Tomorrow, she told herself. Tomorrow.

9

Carysa threatened, "You better wash more'n just your face, Angie, or I'm gonna tell." She stood at the pump, beads of bright water on her shoulders and arms. Angie knew from the way she stood—near the pump spout, hips and feet tensed to start, alert like a rider in a bucking chute—that she wanted to start a water fight. If she said a word, any word, Carysa would throw water onto her, and if Angie tried to catch her she would run to Katla yelling, "Angie didn't wash! Angie didn't wash!" Then Katla would send her back to the pump and Carysa would stick out her tongue. Angie hadn't been Carysa's big sister seven years for nothing; she could read her like a book.

Angie innocently wadded up her washcloth. Then she threw it, hitting Carysa—splat!—right in the face.

"I'm gonna tell," Carysa wailed, striding to the cabin with indignant, long steps that were comical on her short legs. Then Angie washed, splashing the cold water up onto her shoulders and arms until she had to stop or shiver herself apart.

When she went inside, Katla didn't mention the episode

at the pump, so Angie stuck her tongue out at Carysa for a change.

It was like getting ready for a date. Angie had never been on a date, but after listening to Miss Matson talk about dating that's what it seemed like. The girls primped in Katla's bedroom while Dan and Cultus waited for them in the other room. It seemed important for the "men" not to see them until they were all dressed and ready, so Katla acted as their maid, going into the other room for this and that while the girls hid from view through the opening and closing door. Dan and Cultus were good at the game, too. They tried to peek whenever the door opened.

Marta and Angie put on their dresses and straightened all the fringe so it hung right. The buffalo robes were heavy, far heavier than their winter coats, and they fit close over the shoulders like something wet. Only they weren't wet, and the feeling wasn't sticky or uncomfortable at all.

"It feels like a second skin," Angie remarked.

"It is," Marta replied, laughing. "Buffalo skin."

Angie laughed with her, but something turned sour inside of her as they began to braid each other's hair. She remembered the way Lois's face had changed now that her braids were gone. She didn't look like a grasshopper; Angie was sorry she'd ever said that. What Lois's face held now was contempt for herself. It was in the narrowing of her eyes and in the deliberately sharp, flat line of her lips. It was there so forcefully, and not just as a mask, that Angie knew she felt it way down deep inside herself.

Angie's enjoyment of her dress changed almost to shame for the unfairness of it. It had been meant to share.

Their braids were even and tight, and around them the girls wrapped fur braid ties. Angie's and Marta's were otter, and hung down past their waists. The ties made their braids look longer and thicker than they actually were. Carysa's braid ties were white rabbit fur, and shorter. They came down to her shoulders and contrasted cheerfully with her brown cheeks. All three of them wove soft, smoked buckskin around the braid ties to hold them in place on their hair. Then they put on beaded headbands, and, in the back, the single feather that was theirs until they were married.

They put on their best moccasins. Angie's had green and yellow butterflies beaded on the toes, and were high like the ones Katla always wore. Marta laced her new leggin's over her moccasins; they looked like pants cuffs extending from under her dress to the tops of her feet. Angie decided not to wear hers. Remembering Lois again, she was glad they weren't finished.

Finally, they put bead necklaces around their necks and made their appearances. Dan and Cultus whistled in appreciation. And carrying their nicest shawls folded over their arms—Pendleton woolen shawls like the blankets they bought for gifts—they went out to the pickup.

~~~~~~

The loudspeakers on the roof were playing to a thinly filled parking lot when they pulled in, but the Longhouse seemed full—if not yet with crowds of people, at least with the bustle of activity that comes just before the crowds.

Dan and the children marched like a family of ducks, single file behind Katla to their place on the north wall bench. All regular Longhouse people had places along one of the two benches where they always sat. The north wall bench nearest the drummers was Katla's place. It was her territory, and she staked it out so that no one new to the Longhouse would sit there by mistake. The bleachers were for visitors. Katla piled the blankets and cushions along her section of the bench, not attempting to unfold them with her one arm but nevertheless claiming what was hers, while the girls put their shawls over their shoulders and waited for a chance to join the circle.

Steadily the room filled. As she danced, Angie could see whole families come in, everyone carrying a suitcase. She knew what was in the suitcases—costumes—but the families made the Longhouse look a little like a bus station. The afternoon contests were for boys' and girls' war dance, and the rest rooms became packed dressing rooms as parents fussed over their children. The girls emerged dressed much like Angie and Marta, wearing either wing dresses or buffalo dresses, otter braid ties, moccasins, leggin's, shawls, all of it the best they could make, the best they could afford. But the real pageant was put on by the boys. They wore crested headdresses, braid ties, belled spats on their calves, feather bustles and armbands, beaded chokers—all the things their fathers would wear on Sunday when it was the grownups' turn to take a shot at the prize money.

The social dances ended and Angie and Marta were sent to the kitchen. The tables were set up on the dance floor, benches were carried in, and the girls served.

Angie and the other girls her age were setting out venison boiled with *luksh* dumplings, smoked eel, salmon, baked potatoes, boiled roots, mushrooms, fried bread, huckleberries (frozen after last picking season and saved for this weekend), fresh fruit, and baked desserts. The Longhouse cooks had prepared a feast for their friends and guests.

But as greedily as everyone eyed the food, no one began eating out of respect for the Longhouse religion.

The master of ceremonies called on Katla to say the first prayer of the Powwow. Her voice was hardly more than a whisper, but as she began to speak the room was quiet. For a second or two, Angie was troubled by how different Katla looked when she stood to pray. It was a sudden and brief alarm that passed as soon as Angie bowed her head, but in that second or two Katla looked frail. Even in her finery she looked somehow less Indian, less like Katla, as if she were fading. A ghost.

Maybe it was just the white sling that cradled her arm, or maybe it was just her humility in prayer. But Angie had always taken for granted that Katla's strength was limitless— she was so strong that Angie had to resist her. Looking at her for those few short seconds, Angie had the hollow feeling of vulnerability. She bowed her head as Katla began to pray.

Everyone heard her. She asked for a blessing on all who had come and prayed for their happiness and safety. She asked for guidance for the young people, and finally gave thanks for the meal. She closed with the word *chush*, and, as she rang the bell once with her good arm, everyone drank water from the cups in front of them. The meal began.

After they ate, the tables were removed and the floor was swept. Throughout the morning Angie didn't see Lois. She wondered why her friend wasn't there, but she didn't worry; it was a relief to Angie that she wasn't around Cultus.

As the warm-ups for the boys' war-dance contest began, Angie was washing dishes in the kitchen. She didn't see Willie come in with his mother. When Eldon Charley announced the beginning of the contest, she went out with the rest of the kitchen help to watch. That's when she saw

Willie. He was dressed in full costume and was dancing close to the judges. Angie looked around the room until she saw his mother. She looked some more. She couldn't find Lois, but Cultus was in his favorite place, reading comic books.

The Whipman was moving the boys around the floor, encouraging them with words and with his own dancing. Looking out of place among the boys, who were ten years old or under, the Powwow Whipman was what remained of a legend. In the old days, according to Katla, he was the one who taught and disciplined the children. Now all he did was manage the dance floor at Powwows.

The boys were dancing well, Angie thought, especially some of the older ones. The best dancers seemed weightless, rhythmically lifting one foot high while balanced on the other for two or three steps. Moving their feet in this pattern, they crouched, circled, jumped, and danced in figure eights, whooping occasionally to bring their enthusiasm to the attention of the judges. In spite of their best efforts, however, the people in the audience weren't watching the boys. They were watching the Whipman, and like the rest Angie couldn't take her eyes off him.

Jobie Sohappy was reputedly the best dancer on the reservation. In addition, he was young, tall, and slender, and most of the girls Angie's age and older had a crush on him.

The boys respected him, too. He was a tough but understanding reservation policeman, altogether a good choice for Whipman. But the reason everyone watched him was his costume.

Jobie's feathers were orange and blue, his armlets, spats, and bustle matching. He wore no headdress, just two eagle feathers hanging down at an angle from his hair, and very long braid ties. He had a choker around his neck and a bone breastplate. Beneath the breastplate was a bright orange silk shirt, and he had on a blue loincloth to match his feathers—with a black swimsuit underneath. All that gave him an appearance that was hard to overlook.

But that wasn't the main reason he attracted everyone's eyes. He had painted his face. That was seldom done, and Jobie's paint was startling. His face was two colors, split down the middle, so that half of it was brown flesh, the other half orange to match his shirt. The skin-colored half had a jagged white lightning bolt running down the cheek from the corner of his eye and nose. The orange cheek was covered with blue dots the size of dimes.

He would stop sometimes to confer with the judges. Then he would touch some of the boys with the feather in his hand—his whip—to move them closer. Those boys who had the attention of the judges obviously had a chance of winning. Then Jobie would stir the boys up by dancing with them, raising his knees high in order to make the bells on his spats jingle to the beat of the drum.

By the end of the dance the judges had made their selection. After a short time the master of ceremonies announced the winners and presented them with their prizes. Willie Tewet won ten dollars in fourth place. As he walked off the floor Angie approached him.

"Willie," she called out after him. "Willie!" Then catching him by the arm she asked, "What's the matter with you, you deaf?" She chuckled uncomfortably. It was awkward for her to talk with him where everyone could see her.

She felt sillier when Willie wouldn't answer. He looked at the floor in front of his feet with such complete interest that Angie glanced down to see what was there. Nothing.

"Don't pull that wooden Indian stuff on me," she said angrily, losing her chances of finding out anything about Lois.

"Leave me alone," he said, coming out of his trance to scuttle toward the door. Angie turned to watch him go, and saw why Willie had been so anxious to get away from her. Cultus, who had been watching them talk, was now after him. Hardly thinking of what Cultus might do to her, Angie grabbed Willie by the arm again and rushed him out the door, being careful at the same time not to hurt him or ruin any of the feathers on his costume.

105

"He won't hurt you," Angie said to him after they had pushed their way through the people milling around outside the door. She dared him with her tone of voice not to be afraid. Willie sensed the falsehood in what she said.

"Well, everybody says he's gonna hurt us," Willie blurted out. "And Lois is scared of him, too, even if she is trying not to show it." Angie was sure he was about to cry, the way his face squeezed up like a rag being wrung out.

"She didn't mean to break your Katla's arm. Now everybody is being mean to us. Our mother says if Cultus hurts her, she's going to fix him up for good." Willie's face smoothed out as he pronounced the threat. He didn't look like he was going to cry anymore.

"That's what I'm trying to do," Angie said. "I mean, I'm trying to keep Cultus and Lois from getting into a fight."

"Then why aren't you and Lois friends anymore? It looks like you want her to get hurt. Everybody says you don't like Lois anymore 'cause of your Katla. That's what Lois says."

Angie moaned. "You don't understand either," she said. "Listen, Lois won't talk to me—she won't even *look* at me. It's her that don't want to be friends. Every time I see her, she acts stuck up and walks right on by like I was invisible or something. She acts like she's mad at *me*. She broke Katla's arm, not me." Then she knew she had to calm down.

If she wanted Willie to act as her go-between, she had to be sure he took the right message to Lois.

"Look, I want you to tell Lois she's still my best friend. I really feel awful about what happened. It was all Katla's fault, and maybe she just got what she deserved for butting into our business."

"What about Cultus?" he asked. He was beginning to look cold, standing outside in a costume that left most of his skin exposed to the breeze. "What's he going to do? Lois has been hiding around our mother's car. She's afraid that if Cultus sees her he's going to beat her up."

"You just tell her that I'm on her side."

Willie looked cold. Angie could see goose bumps forming, and it occurred to her for the first time why they were called that. Standing there in his war-dance costume, with all his feathers and bare skin, Willie looked partially plucked.

"Okay," he said. With a cadence of bells, he walked back into the building, probably to change. Angie took a searching look for Lois from where she stood, but couldn't see her. Then she went back into the Longhouse, too. She danced in the girls' contest and didn't win.

They stayed at the Longhouse until the drummers gave up, after midnight. She and Carysa had gone to sleep on the bench, but Katla would leave only after she had seen the drummers to their mobile home for the night.

10

The morning came late. Even after they were awake, they talked from their beds, in no hurry to leave the warmth of the blankets or to give up a last chance to doze off one more time. It was Dan who finally said the dreaded words.

"Well, I guess we ought to get up pretty soon," he said, looking at his wrist watch. "It's ten o'clock. I suppose we should get on over there." He had gone to bed with all of his clothes on, except his moccasins. He was in Marta's bed; Marta had to sleep with Katla whenever Dan stayed, which was why he didn't often get an invitation. The cabin was too small for another bed, and Katla said she was too old to have to share.

Dan rolled up on an elbow, looking at them. He didn't seem particularly eager to be the first one up. Angie thought he was probably just hungry, and wanted them to get up and wait on him.

"Nobody's going to be there this morning, anyway," Cultus said, rolling toward the wall and pulling the covers up around himself. "And then even after the worship service, there ain't nobody gonna want to watch a bunch of old raisins waddle around. Why don't we just wait and go tonight?"

Carysa laughed. Partly because she didn't like Carysa laughing when Cultus called old people "raisins," but mostly because there was no chance to go back to sleep, Angie pinched her little sister in a plump spot easily reached under the covers.

"Ow-uch, Angie," she whined. "Why'd you do that? I never done nothin'. Dan, Angie's botherin' for nothin'," she complained, beginning to wrestle.

"It isn't funny, calling people raisins just 'cause they're old," she said, but she was laughing about it too, now, as she tried to keep Carysa from pinching her back. If she was mean to Carysa sometimes it was because somebody had to educate her. She was getting to be too much like Cultus.

Katla stirred them into action as she shuffled through the room. "Cultus, you get the fire started," she said, "and you girls get up and start breakfast." They all got up when they heard her slam the outhouse door the second time, but not before. Just like every other day, that second slam was the alarm clock that meant no further delays in bed were possible because Katla was on her way back up the path.

The Longhouse that Sunday morning had a deserted look, as if it had been raided by vandals who stayed until the cupboards were empty, and who had abandoned the place when the mess became too much to live in. Beneath the benches was an assortment of litter and dirt. Orange peels and apple cores were drying, giving the place a fruity smell that mingled with the smell of juniper smoke from the kitchen. Pop bottles and cans lay about on the hardwood floor, some in the middle of a sticky spill, and wrappers and scraps lay where they'd been dropped beneath the bleachers. An occasional fluff of brightly colored down from someone's costume and beads from a broken string distinguished it as Longhouse litter, but otherwise it was just garbage to Angie.

The disorder of the room made her want to begin cleaning immediately, but when she complained to Katla about it, she was told not to bother cleaning it up yet. "That's part of having company," she said. Looking at it, Angie had a lonely feeling, as if she had been left behind when everyone had moved on.

Katla made the three girls dance; since it was Sunday, half the day's activities were religious. And Cultus had been correct earlier when he had said no one would be there for the worship service.

But the parking lot was full. When Dan parked the pickup that morning Angie had seen Lois's car, looking as if it hadn't been moved overnight. Angie watched for Lois and Willie among the few who wandered in from the parking lot to use the bathroom or raid the kitchen. She expected Willie at least. He might arrange a meeting for the two girls if Lois was too afraid to come into the Longhouse.

Angie danced all seven sevens with sinking hopes. When Willie, Lois, and their mother came in just after the prayer had been said for the meal, it was almost a surprise to Angie. She had been expecting them for so long, and the waiting had been so hard that she was jumpy. Taking a nervous drink from her cup, she choked, couldn't catch her breath, and blushed while Cultus pounded her bruisingly on the back to clear her throat.

Lois was sullen and unkempt, her short hair unparted and hanging unevenly at the sides, and her wing dress wrinkled because, Angie was sure, she'd slept in it. Her dimples, without a smile to shape them, disappeared into dull, long cheeks. But her eyes were alive. Angie could feel them on her. She tried repeatedly to catch them, but they seemed locked on her plate whenever she looked up. Of course, with Cultus sitting next to her, maybe Lois was afraid to look in Angie's direction. Still, Angie could sometimes feel Lois's eyes. The one time Angie managed to look into them and hold them, if only for a fraction of a second, their message was so vague— either with caution because of Cultus or mistrust of Angie— that it only left her more puzzled.

If it hadn't been for the appearance of Mr. Johnson, the

bus driver, in the bleachers just before the raisins danced in the senior citizens' contest, Angie might not have had an unguarded moment in which to sneak up on Lois.

It sometimes happened that white people came to the Jefferson's Day Powwow. There was always the lady from Yakima who owned a bead store. And one of Angie's distant, older cousins was married to a white woman, a sensitive but unattractive person to whom Angie had never spoken. She was in the Longhouse. She had on a pair of moccasins, but her dress looked more like a pioneer's dress than a wing dress, and she never danced or meddled in anything that might turn her in-laws against her.

Aside from her, few whites came to this Powwow, not since the time certain important persons on the Powwow Committee—Katla among them—had been persuaded by a TV station to allow the Powwow to be filmed. The invitations to teachers, ministers, and friends had all abruptly stopped after the uproar that was caused by that film crew. Angie hadn't been old enough to remember it, but she had often heard the story of one young white woman who became so carried away by the drumming that she went out onto the floor with the dancers—to do the twist!

Johnson had probably come to watch the men's war-dance competition. This was the most popular event of the Powwow, with the largest prizes and the largest audience. He sat, much jostled but smiling, at the end of the bleachers, halfway up, nearest the kitchen door.

Cultus was outraged. Angie was in the kitchen when he came in to tell Katla; she had already spotted Johnson and her first thought, like Cultus's, was to tell Katla.

"What's he doing here?" he said, pointing over his shoulder toward the kitchen door with an angry hitchhiker's thumb.

"What's who doing here?" Katla didn't seem to share his wrath, although she certainly did know who he was talking about.

"Them Johnson, the bus driver," he answered bitterly. "He's out there sitting in the bleachers. First he kicks me off the bus, and now he comes to the Powwow. What's he gonna do next?" he insisted.

"So, what's wrong with that?" Katla replied. And Angie agreed with her. He was strange, she admitted, but except for the part about kicking Cultus off the bus, she didn't see what was so wrong with Johnson. Maybe he was just crazy, but that was all. Maybe that's why the boys couldn't drive him crazy—because he already was.

"Well, it just seems we ought to do something about it."

"Now you listen to me, Cultus Wolfe, we ain't gonna do nothin' about it, and you better not do anything about it all by yourself, neither. White people can come to this Longhouse if they wants to. They always have. Since there been white people, anyway."

"Why . . . but . . . this is an Indian place. He's got no business here," he stumbled.

"Cultus," she said in a voice that didn't cover her disgust, "the only time you care about being an Indian is when you need something to hide behind," and she turned away.

There was no disturbance. Katla went out to dance in the warm-ups for the senior citizens' contest. If Johnson had come to watch the men's war dance, he was early, and he was going to have to watch the raisins first. Johnson seemed to have no effect on anyone else.

Except Angie, that is. Seeing Cultus's distraction as her chance to approach Lois, she sneaked up behind her as innocently as she could. She was standing just outside the girls' rest room.

"Meet you outside," she whispered over Lois's shoulder. "In your car." Lois looked a little startled, but then nodded her head. They left the building separately.

Locked safely in the battered green Chevrolet, it seemed as if they had nothing to say to each other. They sat in the back seat looking straight ahead. The windows slowly fogged up. It was Lois who spoke first.

"I like your dress," she said, still looking straight ahead.

"Oh," Angie said, embarrassed rather than flattered. She

114

searched her mind for shortcomings in it. "It's not finished. And I don't have beads or shells. And it don't fit very . . ."

"Mine didn't get finished either," Lois said. "You know, my mom. Oh, she had it sewn together, but then after I did this to my hair, she said I didn't deserve a dress." Saying this, Lois gave her hair an angry pull that had to hurt.

Angie looked into her lap. She hadn't deserved her dress, either, and it wasn't fair. "It'll grow out again, your hair," she said. "Maybe I can trim it for you a little, just sort of even it up. If we do it right it'll be real cute when it's just a little bit longer.

"And next year we'll both have buffalo dresses," Angie vowed, looking up at her friend. "Next year we'll earn them. I'm going to learn how to bead and stuff, and I can help you with yours. Next year we'll have dresses just the same."

"Maybe. Yes, we will. Oh, Angie, what happened?" she said, sliding over to Angie. They held each other, which was awkward sitting side by side on the car seat. Angie didn't care, though. She didn't even care how much her nose was running. It felt good to cry. Katla was right, and she was a crybaby, but so what, she thought.

"Angie, I never meant to do it. It all happened so fast, I don't even know how it happened. It just all sort of built up. I know my hair's ugly and I never should've done it, but she didn't need to say I had lice in front of everybody.

115

"And then, outside, after them McGilvra made me stay in study hall the rest of the day. I was just trying to have some fun with that book. Your Katla slapped me so hard I thought my eye would be black. I just didn't want her to hurt me anymore, and so I was just trying to get away. Then she fell down and broke her arm. Maybe I pushed her, I don't know. I just wanted to get away, that's all."

As Lois talked, Angie tried to comort her. She found herself saying, "It's okay," every time Lois paused. It didn't sound silly; at the time it seemed just the right thing to say.

"After I pushed her I ran across the football field. I stopped once and saw she didn't get up. Everyone was crowded around her like I'd killed her or something, so I just kept on running."

"How did you get home?" Angie asked. She was curious, but more than that she didn't want Lois to stop talking.

"After the bus left, I didn't know how to get home. It was horrible. I went back to the office. The secretary was there. What's her name? The one that looks like a weasel?"

"Mrs. Hutchins?"

"She was still there. That's when I found out I'd broke your Katla's arm. She told me that them McGilvra had to take her to the hospital. Honest to God, Angie, I never meant to break your Katla's arm."

"It's okay. I know you didn't mean to."

"She kept telling me, that weasel lady whatever her name is, that I was really in trouble. She said me and my mom might have to go to court and everything and she made me sit there in the office until them McGilvra got back."

"Boy, I'll bet he was really mad. What did he do?" Angie remembered her own visit to McGilvra's office.

"No, he didn't act mad," Lois answered. "I don't know *why* he wasn't mad at me. He just asked me how it happened, so I told him. Then he asked me a few more questions and said something about this might be one way of learning an important lesson or something. I don't know what he was talking about. I just sat there crying and it was horrible."

"Yeah, that's the way he is," Angie agreed. "You ever been in there before? McGilvra's office?"

"No." Lois shook her head. "He's weird. I don't know about him."

But Angie knew. It was more cruel the way he was always so patient. It would have been easier if he had simply got mad and shouted the time she and Katla were in there. They could have understood that. But McGilvra hadn't even seemed interested.

"So how did you get home?" Angie asked again.

"He asked me if I could ride the activity bus, but I couldn't ride that bus with all those boys. Besides, it only goes as far as Red Salmon and I still couldn't have gotten home."

"I know," Angie said before thinking, "that's why Cultus didn't go out for wrestling." Too late, Angie wished she hadn't mentioned Cultus. Lois pulled away from her and dried her eyes on her sleeve.

"So them McGilvra took me home. I could tell he didn't want to, but he did anyway." There was a long, uncomfortable silence in which Angie tried nervously to think of something to wipe her nose on. Lois's face was clouded over, big thunderheads of consternation building in her brows as she seemed to consider her problems. Angie decided on the back of her hand—she didn't want to smear her dress—by the time Lois renewed the conversation.

"What about Cultus?" she asked. "I mean, what's he going to do? It was bad enough riding to school with you on the bus, not knowing whether you blamed me for what happened."

"I thought *you* were blaming *me* or something," Angie protested. She ended up wiping the back of her hand on her dress anyway. "When you didn't sit with me, or talk to me, or even look . . ."

"I guess I was afraid you wouldn't want me to," Lois interrupted. "You know."

118

"Yeah," Angie said. She didn't know what Cultus was going to do, but she agreed it was scary to think about it. As if Lois's uneasiness were catching, Angie began to worry about getting back before Katla finished dancing. "Listen," she said, "I think I better get back inside before somebody comes looking for me."

"What are we going to do?" She was afraid that Angie was leaving her to face her problems alone.

"Don't worry," Angie said winningly. "I'll see you tomorrow. And if we stick together, I don't think Cultus can beat us both up. You know the way he talks. He won't bother us if we sit on the bus together and everything." She got ready to open the door.

"Can I move back into the locker?" Lois asked timidly. She wasn't looking at Angie, as if she thought she could really say no.

"I'll help you." Angie wanted to hug her friend again, but she got out of the car instead.

Katla won thirty dollars and a blanket. Angie was too late to watch her, so she was left to wonder how Katla could have danced that well with her arm in a sling. Maybe the judges felt sorry for her, she thought, or maybe the contests for senior citizens were like those pet shows where the ugliest dog gets a prize, too.

119

Angie came through the door just as Eldon Charley announced the winners, and it was a good thing she did. When Katla went up to the front of the Longhouse to accept her prizes, Angie and the rest of the children were told to distribute the gifts she had bought. It was typical of Katla to make a point of giving more than she received.

It was dark when the men's contest began, but this was what everyone had come to see. The Longhouse was packed, both with spectators and with dancers.

As in all the dances, an important element in the men's war-dance competition was the dazzle created by color and design and extravagance, but what struck awe in Angie as she watched from the north wall bench was this brilliance swept into motion by the pulse of the drum—loud and close and as vital to her now as her own heartbeat. The stridency of the singers was like a tight, thin wire that stretched and stretched in Angie and threatened to break, sending her to her feet to dance.

The judges would look for a pivot foot that never missed a drumbeat, a pivot foot that shifted while the second foot carved elaborate patterns in the air and on the floor. They would look for spins and crouches and leaps, for bobbing heads and bent bodies close to the floor. They would listen to bells on leggin's as unvarying as the drum, and to the enthusiastic cries of the dancers as they responded to the shrill

120

war song. And yet there was something more important than all of this, and it was what Angie felt as she watched Jobie Sohappy.

This was a man everyone knew, yet who now had eyes that cut right through them, as captivating as the stare of a snake. There was no mistaking that here was a man about to kill. Most importantly, war dancers were judged on their ability to create this drama.

Not many people could watch that dance and be still. The excitement on the floor gave energy to the spectators and Angie could see Cultus among those crowded around the kitchen. He was standing behind several others but from the way his head swayed Angie knew that he was bending at the knees and moving his feet to the rhythm of the drum. It was the seriousness of the war dance—the intimidation that characterized it—that appealed to Cultus, she thought, and his face had an expression much like Jobie's.

As Angie could have foreseen, Jobie Sohappy won first prize and Uncle Dan made a fool of himself. She was glad when Dan was eliminated early, so she could allow the enchantment of the dance to take her completely.

Dan had a wig he liked to wear when he danced, since he kept his hair cut too short for braids. In one of his more spirited tries to swing his paunch around, he jerked his head too fast, upsetting the wig. It rotated on his head so that one

121

of the braids hung down the middle of his face, causing good-humored laughter. He was such a clown, Angie would have bet he had done it on purpose. Dan didn't win anything.

The Powwow planners had, of course, saved the best until last for a reason. And with the men's competition over and the winners announced, the Longhouse emptied as fast as a football stadium. There was one final meal, but it was late and even the drummers didn't stay for it. It was a long way back to Crow. Dan set up one table. And after they had eaten, he didn't take it down. The girls stacked the dishes on the kitchen counter but didn't wash them because Katla, looking the place over, said, "Come on, let's go. We can clean this mess up some other time."

Powwow was over.

Angie found herself, as she surveyed the empty room, over-come with a longing for the security of her whole family, close under one roof. She was glad, after they got home and had started the fire in the stove, when Dan decided to stay. Katla was relaxed and talkative as she sat with her chair tilted back against the wall. The fire in the stove cast shadows on the ceilings and walls; not wild, war-dancing shadows, but silent, embracing ones with eyes and smiles of light opening up in them. Angie lay on her side, looking through half-closed lids at the friendly shapes in the room. Curled up be-side her and facing the wall, Carysa had gone to sleep. She stirred often, sleeping poorly in the overheated room. Angie could feel the heat from the stove through the bedclothes. She was as content as a cat.

Dan, lying on top of Marta's bed on his back, still had his clothes on, even his moccasins. He was watching the light show on the ceiling. Cultus sat on his bed with his back against the wall and with his knees drawn up under his chin. Marta was slumped in a chair at the table. There was a wholeness to the group which was as warming to Angie as the stove.

Nobody said, "Tell us a story," but it was the perfect time for one. When Katla began to talk, her words were harmonious with Angie's mood and with the warmth of the room and the sound of the fire, with the evening.

"This is a story my Katla used to tell me, Cultus. I heard her tell it to me many times. I want you to listen well. There's something you can learn from it.

"This is not a story about Coyote the Trickster or how Cottontail lost his long bushy tail or any of those. I've told you all of those stories, and you know them by now. I want to tell you a story about our people when my Katla was just a little girl.

"It wasn't always the whites who threatened our way of life. In my Katla's time and before that it was some of those people who war danced with us today—or, what I mean is, it was their ancestors. They were our enemies. Not the white man.

"None of you ever knew my Katla. She was an old, old woman when I was just so high, and when I was only eight or nine she died. Some said she was over one hundred years old. I don't know. But she was so old she was skinny and bent like a juniper tree, and her face was like bark, so wrinkled. She was blind when I was a little girl, so I had to take her places. She was an old, old woman.

"She walked with a stick. Not a cane, but a long stick. I remember that because sometimes I would take her someplace and she would fall down. Then she would try to hit me with the stick, but she couldn't do it because she couldn't see.

"She had to walk with this stick because she was blind, and because of her foot, too. She walked with a limp where she had been shot in the foot with an arrow. They used to hide in caves in the river cliffs or in holes in the ground and pull brush over themselves when the Paiutes would come to kill and rob. They were our enemies then, and they shot my Katla in the foot so that she limped all her life.

"They were our enemies then. Not the white man. My Katla used to tell me this story, when I was just a little tiny girl, about the first white men to come to the place now called Sherar's Bridge.

124

"Our people knew they were coming, even though no one had told them they were on their way. Now some had seen white men before, on the Columbia River. There was one old man who died many, many years ago who saw Lewis and Clark. He remembered because there was a black man with them, the first anyone had ever seen. But that's another story.

"At that time we just lived in our little valley. That word, *tygh*, 'little valley,' is what the white men named us when they came there to settle. We spent every winter there, and went to fish at the falls on the Deschutes just like we still do. Now the dams have covered up the great falls on the Columbia where we used to fish, but we still have the place on the Deschutes named Sherar's Bridge by the white men. But before any white men had been there, we knew that they were coming.

"This is how we knew ahead of time that the white men were coming: The old people of our band had a dream. In the dream people who needed help came to them. They had eyes like stars and they brought strange things with them.

"They had one thing that you could put a fire into and it wouldn't burn the thing up. You could take it into a teepee and it would make the teepee warm but there would be no smoke because the fire was inside this thing. My Katla used to tell me that the thing in the dream was a stove.

125

"We didn't have metal. We didn't even have pans. This is how we had to cook everything: We made water-tight baskets out of cedar roots, and cooked our meat by boiling it in these baskets. You couldn't put the basket on the fire or it would burn up. We heated the water by dropping hot, round rocks from the fire into the basket. That's how we used to cook, so in the dream the thing that held fire was something no one had seen.

"Also in the dream the people with eyes like stars had another thing that was made of metal. They took this thing and stood beside a tree. Pretty soon the tree fell down. They stood beside another one, and after a while it fell down, too. They were told that this would be a good thing for them, and they shouldn't be afraid of it. I guess this was a saw.

"According to the dream, the newcomers had three things. The last one was a thing you laid flat and then you looked into it. When you looked into it, it talked to you. My Katla said this thing was the Bible.

"And so when the white men first came to Sherar's Bridge we didn't fight them and we didn't run away and hide like from our enemies, the Paiutes.

"At first, they couldn't even get down to the river. It was the best place to get down. That's why the road goes there now. Everywhere else along there, just cliffs. But it was still so steep they couldn't get the wagons down, and nothing on the hills but sagebrush. The white people couldn't lower the wagons because there was nothing to tie their ropes to.

"So the men, Indian men, tied ropes to their saddles and lowered the wagons with their horses. Our saddles then weren't like the white men's saddles. Ours were made from deer and elk horns, and they tied the ropes to these. It took many horses, and they let the wagons down one at a time without losing any of them.

"After they were at the bottom of the canyon, of course, they couldn't get across the rapids. The women began making Indian ropes. They made rope from the bark of the willows that grow along the river there. It was the same kind of rope that our people used to make fishing nets out of. To make the ropes they rolled the bark like this on their thighs."

Katla, still leaning back in her chair, rubbed her palm over her thigh back and forth several times. "My Katla used to show us her thigh when she told us this story. It was all scars from having to make ropes like this. All the old women had scars like this from having to make rope, but there was no other way.

"They used this rope that they made to tie a bridge across the narrowest part of the rapids, where the cliffs are so close together that a good man on a good horse could jump across

127

the river. I myself have seen this done, but only once. Many died trying. To fall in the water there is to die. It was just above where the highway bridge is now.

"This rope bridge wasn't really a bridge at all. Just some ropes to walk on and some to hold on to. They didn't plan to take the wagons across here. But the women and children crossed the falls because it was safer than fording the river with the wagons.

"They tied one rope around the middle of each person as they went across the bridge. That way they hoped to pull them out if the bridge broke. They went across one at a time.

"When the women and children were across on the easy side of the canyon, they walked along the river. On the other side, the wagons made their dangerous trip through the cliffs. Many times they had to be raised and lowered with the horses, and all the while up above them the canyon walls towered where the earth was broken.

"When they came to a wide place in the river, where the water ran the slowest, they began to float the wagons across. Once again we helped them with our horses. The men guided the wagons across by tying the horses to them and swimming them across.

"Everyone got across the river safely. Our people then guided the whites the rest of the way into central Oregon. When they were settled, we returned to our own valley.

128

This was the first time we helped the whites. It was not the only time. My own father fought in their wars against other Indians. The white men were not our enemies."

Katla grew silent and distant as Angie waited for the soaring sensation that would take her away to sleep. Cultus had long ago stretched out on his bed and gone to sleep; if Katla's story about the wagons was intended to teach him something, it had been lost on him. Dan, on his back on Marta's bed, was not quite snoring, but he was gasping and snorting in a way that was worse. Just as Angie drifted off there was the fleeting vision of her own face looking down on her body as it slept.

~~~~~~

11

It was more like getting ready for school after a vacation than after a weekend. There was a foreign quality about the morning. Angie reflected that it had been four days, not two, since she had been to school. It seemed silly, however, that it took so much effort to remember the schedule of her classes.

It was even more like the end of a vacation for Cultus. He had missed one whole week, and now he sounded just the way he always did at the end of summer or Christmas.

"I ain't goin'," he said when Katla came back into the house after her usual morning trip. She looked a little surprised at this. The girls were getting dressed. They had gotten up when the door slammed the second time, as usual. Without a response of any kind Katla went to the stove and squatted with a groan, as if to get the fire started.

She had soot on her cast before Marta asked to do it for her. When the old woman straightened up again, with an identical groan, she had a piece of stove wood in her hand.

"Get out of bed, Cultus," she said.

Cultus repeated himself with a sidelong glance at Katla

that made Angie scared. It was insolent and challenging. "I ain't goin'," he said. His eyes said, Make me!

"Get out of bed," Katla said again with a ripple like raised hair in her voice. There was no doubt in anyone's mind that she meant to use that piece of wood if she had to.

"All right, all right," Cultus laughed uneasily. "Can't you take a joke?"

They were walking to the road in plenty of time this morning. Katla was worried that the bus might not wait for them, since they hadn't ridden it for a couple of days. She herded them down the road in front of her, stick of firewood still in her hand, like a drove of balky cows. She was going along to make sure that Cultus got on the bus.

As the five of them clomped along, a meadowlark flew from the grass beside the road. Angie watched it land on a fence post, yellow V-necked sweater on its breast. She didn't know whether it had been singing or not; if it had been, she'd missed it because she only noticed it as it flew.

"What is the lark supposed to say when it tells you your future?" she asked. Katla was about three steps behind her.

"I don't know. It's your future," she replied, grumpy, then added in a mellowing voice, "You have to listen for yourself, Angie."

It would sure be a lot easier, she decided, if you could find out your future in a vision, where you could see everything nice and clear, like the Indians in the legend of Sherar's Bridge.

They got to the road. Katla regarded them coldly from some distance, staying back so she wouldn't have to speak to Johnson. It didn't work. When the bus pulled to a stop, its engine died. Johnson got out, saying hello to her. Katla, seeing that Cultus was on the bus, grunted a wordless, rude response. She threw the stick down and turned back up the road.

Johnson opened the hood. Wiggled the battery cables. Slammed the hood shut again. The bus cleared its raw throat for several seconds, and started.

It was a nice day, clear and bright. Angie looked out the window to where the great snowy peaks of the high Cascades poked up like the backbone of a skinny horse. She thought she could spot the meadows where she picked huckleberries every summer on the flanks of Pahtu, the mountain. The whites had named it Mt. Jefferson.

That got her to thinking, and her mind roamed with the view. It occurred to her that this was her land. It started above the barren white of Pahtu, at its summit, and fell to the green of timberline and further, to where that green gave way to the more familiar color of the plains—earthy browns and yellows dotted with sage and juniper, green again but duller. It was almost like an independent country, the reservation, with its own laws, its own flag, language, and people.

132

Everything but its own high school. This was her land, but every day she left it to go to school in Baker.

Angie was glad when Lois boarded the bus. She didn't like the drift of her thoughts. They were too much like something Cultus might think.

"Hi, Angie," she said, sitting down. Angie didn't think she'd ever seen Lois *sit* down on the bus before.

After sitting, she slid so low in the seat that her knees were higher than her head. "One of these days you're going to break your back, sitting like that," Angie teased. Then she slid into the same posture. But it was too uncomfortable to stay scrunched up like that for long, and after the first few bumps they sat up a little.

"I don't want Cultus spyin' on us," she said. "Did he say anything? About me, I mean?" Lois was talking so quietly that it was hard for Angie to hear. She kept having to say "Huh?" and that was annoying for both for them.

When Angie understood Lois's question she looked at her friend with narrowed eyes. She had a sudden suspicion that Lois was going to use this mess to flirt with Cultus. Maybe the whole thing was just one big flirt.

"No," she answered. "He didn't say anything about you. He's too busy looking for trouble. I think he's forgotten all about it and he's looking for some way to get kicked off the bus again."

"How come?"

"He wants to drop out of school, and Katla won't let him. So he thinks that if he gets kicked off the bus he won't have to go anymore. He won't have time to bother you."

"Man, I hope so," she said, but not very persuasively. Angie thought she detected a strain of disappointment in her voice.

"Boy, I'm never going to do that again, though," she added after a moment's silence. Angie was about to ask what, when Lois said, "I mean, next time I'm just gonna let her slap my eyes out."

At school, Angie wasn't able to stick with Lois every minute the way she'd planned. Indian students had so many unexcused absences that teachers automatically refused to accept late assignments without a note. The rule went for white students, too, but they weren't expected to dance three days and nights at funeral ceremonies. They didn't have to harvest roots during those few short weeks in spring, but they did have mothers who could write excuses. Angie didn't have an excuse from home, but she stayed after every class to try to get her make-up work.

Even though Miss Matson was Angie's favorite teacher, it wasn't any easier to get back assignments in Health than it was for any other class. When Angie went to Health on Monday she found out that she'd missed a quiz on Friday and her grade, because her absence was unexcused, was an F. Miss Matson liked to write scores on the board following

134

tests and quizzes, and Angie noticed that three other girls had the same failing grade, all Indian girls. Many Indian parents expected their children to help them get ready for the Powwow. Angie stayed after the bell, but when she heard Miss Matson refuse to let Elsie Mitchell make up the quiz, she decided to come back at noon to talk with the teacher.

They were eating when Angie asked Lois, "Why didn't you tell me there was a quiz on Friday. Can I see your paper?" Since it was an emergency, it wasn't quite the same as cheating.

"I don't have it. She didn't let us keep them. There were too many kids gone, so she just went over it after she picked up the papers. Anyway, what difference does it make? She won't let you make it up."

"She knows Katla, and maybe if I explain to her that Katla can't write she'll let me take the quiz."

"Not because of no Powwow she won't. You know that."

"Well, I can try. Can you remember what was on the quiz? What were the questions about?"

"Oh, you know. That stuff from chapter seven, about manners and stuff."

"Was there a question about poise?" Getting information from Lois was like a fill-in quiz itself—you had to put the words in the blank spaces.

"I think so. I'm not sure. The whole test was hard for me. I got the lowest grade in the whole class, next to you. I don't like quizzes anyway. You wanna eat my sandwich?" Lois didn't like toasted tuna fish, either.

"Okay," Angie said, reaching for the sandwich. "I guess I can't go to intramurals with you. I'm going to see Miss Matson after lunch. I've got to talk her into letting me take that test. I had an A in that class until this happened."

"She won't let you do it," Lois said. She looked disappointed, then thoughtful. "Guess I'll go to the library, then," she said.

"The library?" Angie was surprised. "Since when do you go to the library during lunch hour? You've never done that before!"

"Well, you know, Cultus always goes to the game at noon," she explained. "I don't think I better . . ."

"Yeah. Well, see you later, then."

Angie went to the hall outside the teachers' room and waited until Miss Matson came out carrying her lunch sack and a thermos bottle.

"Oh, hi, Angie. Did you want to see me?" she said, putting her free arm around Angie's shoulders. Angie explained why she had missed school the previous week as they walked back to Miss Matson's classroom, but the teacher didn't change her mind.

"I'm sorry, sweetheart, but I can't let you make it up. It's the rule, and it wouldn't be fair to the others if I made an exception for you. We just can't let our students miss school for every little thing, and maybe you'll try harder to get to school next time if you have this to remind you of what can happen. I really am sorry." She sounded sorry, too, but Angie came away depressed and angry.

"It ain't fair," Angie grumped to Lois later. They were waiting for the bus after school. "I had an A!"

"I told you she wouldn't let you take the test. We should've gone to the basketball game."

"Did you go to the library?" Angie asked. She had, and not only that. Lois had checked out some books. Angie asked to see them as they stood on the sidewalk waiting for the bus.

"Why did you pick these?" Angie asked, flipping through one of them while she cradled the other two in her elbow. They were books about Indians. The library had a whole section of Indian books, since about a third of the kids in school were Indian.

Lois replied honestly. "Because of the pictures. Look here," she said, taking the book back from Angie and finding a page. "This one's got stuff on how to do beadwork." She showed Angie a drawing of the type of loom used to make beaded belts, like the belt Angie had from her mother.

"Why, you big dope," Angie said, laughing, until she saw Lois was hurt by it. Then she added, "You don't need this book to teach you how to bead. Probably written by some white woman, anyway. Why don't you just ask your mom?"

Angie and Lois weren't standing in their usual places. It

137

seemed to them that they were always either on the bus or waiting in line for it; today they had stopped to look at the books and the line had formed without them. When the bus pulled up they were at the back. They didn't see Cultus come up behind them.

He came out of the school building, dawdling in his usual manner—with his empty hands in his pockets—but seeing Lois in an open spot he rushed to the line as if he had been called. About the only time Cultus looked boyish was when he concentrated on something. He had that look on his face now, but anyone seeing him would have stepped aside. The only thing Cultus ever concentrated on that hard was trouble.

But Lois didn't see him coming.

Cultus pushed her. She fell forward, the book dropping, and landed on her hands and knees. Cultus elbowed past a couple more kids and stopped. Mr. Johnson, who had seen it all, was just getting up from the driver's seat.

"You big bully," Angie shouted. She was sputtering, unable to think or talk straight. "You're nothing but a big, dumb idiot. I wish somebody'd knock your block off," she managed to say, but she was almost instantly sorry she had.

Cultus raised his arm as if to let her have it, and it wasn't until she'd blinked and dropped the other two books like a fool that she realized he wasn't really going to hit her. "What are you sticking up for her for?" he asked. "She broke Katla's arm. And besides," he added with a grin, "I never meant to push her. I was gonna miss the bus. It was an accident."

"She didn't mean to break Katla's arm, either. Katla slapped her. If someone slapped you, you'd break their neck!"

Behind them Johnson was saying, "Look out. Get out of my way," as he tried to get through the kind of clump kids make when they want to watch a fight. Lois was sitting on the ground, holding a knee and crying silently. Angie tried to help her up, but Lois didn't want to get up.

She thought she could see a look of concern for Lois flicker in Cultus's eyes as he looked down at her. It hadn't been Lois he was after. Everything was squared between them, but when Johnson butted in like a silly goat, the nightmare continued.

"I saw you do that!" he said, hardly able to speak. His face was as red as a tick, gorged with blood and about to burst. "I saw you do that, Cultus!"

"Yeah, and what are you going to do about it, white man?" he snarled, swelling to about twice his size like a frog.

"Cultus!" Angie was trying to sound threatening, trying to let him know she would tell on him. But her voice had cracked and Cultus ignored her. Then Lois spoke.

"It was an accident, Mr. Johnson. Honest. And I'm not hurt at all. I just skinned my knee a little when I tripped."

To prove it she stood up, but couldn't resist a dramatic little grimace. Neither Cultus nor Johnson seemed to care.

"Well," Cultus menaced, "what you gonna do?"

Angie knew this was a challenge that the bus driver couldn't back away from. If he did, Cultus wouldn't ride the bus, he would ride the driver. Angie also knew that to take up the challenge would mean a fist fight.

"I'm takin' you to the office, that's what I'm gonna do about it." Some of the color was out of his face.

"You gonna make me?" Cultus dared. " 'Cause I don't think you can."

"I don't think I have to make you," Johnson replied. His face was back to its normal color—faded carrot—and his voice was full of forbearance. He's going to try to be understanding again, Angie thought. It was the wrong thing to say in a situation where there was no right thing to say. Cultus took a swing at the bus driver that would have sent him to the moon if it had connected. It didn't. Johnson, in control of himself now, easily avoided the blow, stepping back on Tammy Niner's foot as he did so.

"Ow-uch," she complained, but nobody heard her. Everyone watched Cultus run across the football field. He looked just like Lois had, and Angie thought that it could easily have been a rerun from last week. The whole thing was silly.

140

"Everybody get back on the bus," Johnson ordered as soon as Cultus was out of sight. They went.

Later, on the bus, Angie observed that it had seldom been so quiet. "What did he do it for?" Lois asked, and in the same breath, "I wonder where he is now?" To Angie, it was beginning to sound a lot like a crush. She shook her head. It was just crazy. She stared out the window at the simple, white permanence of Pahtu, a little washed out now against the afternoon dullness of a changing April sky.

———

It was almost as if Angie had tried to hit the bus driver herself, the way Katla snapped at her. With that kind of treatment, Angie wasn't exactly eager to volunteer information. She told herself that there was no reason to worry Katla with more than she knew absolutely was true.

"Where is he then, if he didn't come home on the bus?" Katla asked angrily. Now Angie was responsible for leaving him somewhere, that's the way she made it sound.

"I don't know," she answered. "He just ran away like I told you. How am I supposed to know where he went?"

Angie was rinsing the dinner dishes when a car came up the road. Dan drove fast, but not this fast. He wouldn't have dared. His pickup would have fallen apart.

Jobie Sohappy was behind the wheel of his police car with Cultus beside him in the front seat. Angie didn't want to look foolish in front of Jobie, but she couldn't help herself; she dropped the dishes with a clatter and ran back into the house.

"Katla, there's a . . ." she started to say, but then she decided to keep quiet. Katla had a cornered look. She got out of the way, then stood watching from a safe distance.

"What's he done, my boy?" Katla asked in English as Jobie walked up. Angie thought to herself that he was every bit as handsome in his uniform as he had been as Whipman at the Powwow. The stripe on his pantleg made him look even taller and more slender. And he didn't look afraid of Katla. Before he spoke, he took off the white Stetson hat that was part of his uniform.

"*Ai,*" he said, giving Katla the Indian greeting. And Katla repeated her question, this time in Indian.

"What did Cultus do now?" she said. "Or are you just bringing him home because he missed the bus?" Her voice sounded hopeless, in spite of the question.

"Well, yes, I am just bringing him home, for a while, but I'm afraid that he's going to have to go back with me. I'm sorry, but Cultus got into a little trouble this afternoon, and we're going to have to keep him in the Group Home for a few days. Probably not for long, but at least until he begins to feel a little better about a few things that seem to be troubling him."

Marta began to cry quietly. Angie wondered if she should

142

be crying, too. After all, she was the crybaby, not Marta. But somehow, coming from Jobie bad news didn't seem quite as bad. Angie figured that Jobie could tell her that the world was going to end in five minutes and she would be glad to hear it.

"Do you mean that taking a punch at the bus driver is so bad that you got to take my grandson away from me? He didn't even hit him, did he?"

"I don't think they're going to take him away from you. He'll probably only be down there a couple of weeks. You see, taking a swing at the bus driver isn't all that we think Cultus did this afternoon." Here Jobie seemed to be considering his words very carefully before he spoke, but he didn't look at the ground or off into space as he did so. He looked right into Katla's eyes, as if trying to see how she would take the news.

"I got a call this afternoon from the sheriff's office in Baker. They'd picked him up. They had him in a cell when I got there."

"In a cell!" Katla's eyes blazed. "Not for hitting a bus driver, they didn't. Now you tell me, what did he do?" she demanded. Her patience was worn out; she didn't want to be spared or have the news broken to her gently. But when Jobie told her, she wilted.

"He stole a car. We think," Jobie answered. "It seems that about five minutes to four, the sheriff got a call from a

143

man saying that a boy had taken his pickup. He had left it running while he went into the post office. That's against the law, to leave your car running, and he got a ticket for it even if his car was stolen. But still, somebody took it, and he said it was an Indian boy.

"Then about five minutes after that, the sheriff got another call. This time it was about somebody wrecking a pickup. It turned out to be the same one, and Cultus was in it. He wasn't hurt or anything. He tried to pull out in front of some other cars, to cross an intersection. I guess Cultus doesn't know how to drive yet?" he asked.

Katla shook her head no.

"Anyway, he killed the engine when he tried to pull out. Another car hit him. When the sheriff got there, Cultus was sitting on the curb looking at the mess he'd gotten himself into."

"What does Cultus say?" Katla asked, probably thinking he would deny it. Cultus was still in the police car, either because Jobie had told him to stay there or because he had been scared to face Katla. Now Jobie turned and called him from the car with a wave of his arm.

"Oh, he says he did it, all right. You want to ask him about it?" As Cultus came sheepishly toward them, Jobie said in a confidential tone, "He's pretty upset about it." Then he stepped back to Cultus and encouragingly put his arm around his broad, blocky shoulders.

144

"Did you do that, Cultus, what Jobie says?" she asked, sounding as if she wished he would say no. Cultus just shrugged and looked at the ground. "I've raised over thirty children, most of them not my own. And Cultus, I swear you can get into more trouble than all of them put together," she said with a wry face, as if she was almost amused. "Why did you do it?"

"I dunno," he said, barely loud enough to be heard. "I guess it was because I wanted to come home. I was just walking around, and then there it was—the pickup—so I took it."

Now Angie began to cry, no sobs, just a couple of nearly dry drops from each eye. He was lying. Cultus was always so dumb. He couldn't put up with anything he didn't like. He always had to do something about it, and it was always the wrong thing.

"Well, he's a little confused right now," Jobie said, patting him a couple of times on the shoulder. "As soon as we get this thing sorted out, he'll be back home to stay. Right now, what he needs to do is to get some clothes and things packed up, so he'll have something to wear. Why don't you girls go with him and help him pack what he needs, okay? I'd like a chance to talk with your Katla for a minute or two."

That meant that they had to miss the best part—the part they weren't supposed to hear. The girls were disappointed, but they didn't complain. Reluctantly, they followed Cultus into the cabin.

145

He sat down immediately, chin resting in his hands, and stared at the floor between his feet. For a long time no one spoke and no one made any effort to pack his things.

Carysa, as could be expected, was the one to break the silence with a silly question. "Was it fun to steal a car, Cultus?" she asked, curious and not just smarty. Cultus didn't answer. He just made a sound through his nose that was impossible to interpret as either a yes or no. The hush that followed was so awkward that everyone but Cultus fidgeted. Finally he spoke.

Forgetting Carysa's question, he asked, "How's Lois? I mean, she wasn't really hurt or anything, was she?"

"If you didn't want to hurt her, why did you push her?" Angie asked brutally, knowing all the time what the answer was. Maybe she just wanted to see if Cultus knew why he had done it.

"I don't know. I guess I just go crazy sometimes. You know, I wasn't really mad at her about Katla's arm. I guess I never really was. Tell her that, will ya?"

Angie agreed with a nod to do so, although Lois already knew. Angie was sure of it. That's why Lois stuck up for Cultus when Johnson charged off the bus after him. There was never any real problem between Lois and Cultus.

"I'll tell her," Angie said. "Are you still gonna have to go to school?" she asked. She took his toothbrush and comb from the windowsill and put them in a paper sack. Marta

146

was putting underclothes in another sack while Carysa held it open for her. Cultus sat in the same position on the edge of his bed.

"Nobody told me yet," he answered. "I don't know how I can without riding the bus. And I bet I never have to ride that bus again." He seemed satisfied.

"Where were you goin' to run to with that truck?" Marta asked. "You were lyin' when you said you were coming back here." Just as Carysa could always pick up a fallen conversation with her silliness, it was always Marta who dropped it back to earth with her blunt honesty. Cultus looked at her with knowing eyes.

"I dunno," he said. "Portland, maybe."

"You had a plan, right?" Marta was being nasty. "You had it all worked out. You were going to leave this reservation with its backward Indians and go to the big city, just like our father did. And die of drinking, just like he did and their mother did and how many others? Cultus, the only backward Indian around here is you!"

Angie was surprised that Marta could say that and get away with it. The bruise on her own arm had just turned from purple to violet, and she wouldn't forget what had happened between her and Cultus for a long time. But Marta seemed to be reading her brother's mood correctly. He didn't like what she said, but he seemed to take it as due to him.

"Well, I had to do something."

"Why? Why are you so much better than the rest of us?"

"Listen. Them McGilvra told me there ain't no way I can graduate from that high school. He won't come right out and say that I'm a stupid Indian, but that's what he means. Why should I waste my time going in there, then? It's all the time reading those baby books and listening to some English teacher tell me . . ."

"Yeah, well you listen to me, too," Marta interrupted. Angie had never seen her this angry before, and Carysa looked at her with surprise and maybe a little fear in her eyes. Marta was every bit as big as Cultus, and if there was going to be a fight it was going to be a good one. "All this trouble you cause is your own fault. You're the only one out to get Cultus Wolfe."

She stopped with that and turned away. With quick, angry exactness she folded Cultus's shirts on the table and put them into the same sack with his underwear. There was rage in Cultus's eyes, but for a long time he didn't move. There was a silence, like before a cat leaps.

Cultus stood and Angie's throat tightened, but he said, "Jobie's waiting."

Marta turned to him, holding the sack out. "Can't you see how hard we're trying?" she sputtered.

Cultus hung his head and took the sack. As soon as it was out of her hand, Marta hugged her brother.

And Cultus hugged back.

12

Cultus did have to go to school. He was headed into the principal's office with Jobie when Angie and Lois walked into the building on Tuesday. The policeman was so natural and self-possessed as he waved to them that Angie felt relaxed and collected, too.

Even Cultus looked as if he were in high spirits, but Angie pitied him, knowing where he was going. She knew how McGilvra would treat him—with so much understanding that Cultus would choke on it. He would tell him that he wasn't bad because he had stolen a car, or because he had tried to hit the bus driver, or pushed Lois, or even because he was Indian. But Cultus would still feel like he was bad. McGilvra would act like he really knew why Cultus was bad, but wasn't telling him because he was a kid and shouldn't know about such things. Being a kid was like having a disease that was going to kill you. Cultus would be the only one who didn't know he had it, and he would feel that everybody was keeping something from him.

"What are they going to do to him, do you know?" Lois asked after he and Jobie disappeared into McGilvra's office.

They watched Mrs. Hutchins leave the office counter, where she had been selling lunch tickets to a line of kids, and gently close the door behind Jobie.

"I'm not sure yet," Angie answered. "Katla didn't say, except that we got to go to court about it."

"They're not going to send him to reform school or anything, are they?"

"What does it matter to you?" Angie teased her friend. Out of the corner of her eye she could see Lois blush.

"It doesn't matter to me at all," she protested with a pout. "Just curious. Can't I even ask? When does he go to court?"

"I think Katla said Monday. Jobie wouldn't let us listen when he told her about it. But don't worry. I have to go, too, so I'll tell you everything. Everybody has to go, Dan too."

Angie wasn't teasing now. Her voice was serious. "Dan said they might try to take us away from Katla."

"Aw, they always say that," Lois said knowingly. "Every time my mom runs off, me and Willie have to go to court, too. They haven't done it yet—take us away from her. All they do is keep us in the Group Home until she sobers up."

"Dan says they think Katla is too old to take care of us."

"What else can they do with you? Your mom and dad are dead, and they sure ain't gonna put you in the Group Home for the rest of your life." Angie wasn't reassured. She knew both of them—Dan and Lois—well enough to know they could be mistaken.

At home it was as if something had punched a big hole in the wall of the cabin. Angie would never have believed she could miss Cultus, but his absence was something they all tried to step around like a draft too big to stop up.

He'd only been gone from home two days when Katla said to them, "You know, even after all this many children, I still can't let them go. I miss him already like he was gone." Everyone knew what she meant by "gone." Katla believed that ghosts came in the house whenever the wind blew a window or a door ajar.

That same evening they all drove into Red Salmon with Dan to see Cultus.

The Group Home was made out of brick. It had a large porch with huge white pillars—four of them—and a balcony, but these two features didn't help; as if built by the third little pig, it was made to be solid, and it was as unattractive and as stark as it could be. It was the building that had been the boys' dormitory during the boarding school days.

Dan hesitated outside it, saying, "I've done my time already. I don't want to go back in there.

"I was here for eight years," he said. "It took me that long to get through the sixth grade, and that wasn't slow for them days. But that's as far as I got.

"They used to have a flagpole out there." He stopped, pointing to a field that now had a baseball diamond on it.

Everybody stopped to listen. "We always had to march out there—rain or shine, through snow if it was on the ground—and do this flag raisin' thing. Every day. We had to march in rows of three in a long line. Everybody had to walk with the same foot at the same time, like in a parade, or they'd holler at you.

"We called it the Trail of Tears, but not where anybody could hear us, any of them teachers. You had to be real careful. When I came down here in the first grade I couldn't talk English. And them teachers, they'd make you stand up against the chalkboard with your nose in a circle for talkin' Indian. If they caught you whisperin' in Indian in this dormitory, they'd give you a whippin'.

"And we all wore braids when we came. But when we was down here, after three days they cut off your hair like this." Dan showed them with three movements of his hand, a cut across the bangs and each side. Just like Lois's haircut, Angie thought. If he objected to this, she was curious why Dan kept his hair cut so short now. "They said we all had bugs, that's why they cut it.

"And we all wore moccasins when we came. But they wouldn't let us wear them in school. They had these shoes like canoes we had to wear. Every year when we'd come down out of the hills for school, the teacher would give me a pair of shoes to wear, but they gave me blisters. They'd always tell me they had ordered different ones in the mail, but they never came.

"I did my time here. And I don't like it, coming back."

Dan asked an unfriendly white man at a desk where Cultus Wolfe was. He looked them over suspiciously, it seemed to Angie. She wondered if he was going to take them back and unlock the door or whatever, but he only said, "Room eight, three doors down and on the left."

Cultus greeted them without enthusiasm. He was sitting on a couch which also must have been someone's bed. A sheet was wadded into one corner of it, and Cultus had his feet tucked under a wool blanket. The room contained half a dozen other unmade beds, some with boys in them. One was reading a book. The others were absorbed, like Cultus, in a bloody police story on the television set.

Angie was uncomfortable. She felt like she'd walked into the boys' locker room at school or something. There were clothes on the floor and a couple of boys were lounging in their underwear. She had a distinct feeling of shame, as if she shouldn't be here, but try as hard as she could to keep her eyes down, she caught herself looking at them with far more curiosity than she'd ever felt for Cultus.

Besides, the appearance of the room was discomforting in itself. There were screens on the windows, not the kind to keep bugs out, but people in. There was even a locked box over the TV dial. She looked to see if there was a lock on the door. It looked like a regular handle, but Angie decided that was only to make it look as if it wasn't a jail. It felt like one, though.

It would have been impossible to talk over the racket of the television, and no one tried. They surrendered to it instead. Angie found it difficult to pick up the story, coming into it in the middle of the program, but she enjoyed the movie that came on next—a western with no Indians in it.

She lay on the floor with Carysa. The others shared the couch with Cultus, shoulder to shoulder, and the whole family stared hypnotized and unmoving through the movie and commercials alike. It was well into the eleven o'clock news before the sour man from the desk came in and turned off the set.

"You have everything you need?" Katla asked Cultus after the room grew quiet enough to talk. He yawned before he said he guessed so.

"Well, I think we'd better get on home now," Dan said, standing. "Tomorrow's a school day. You take it easy, Cultus."

"Yeah." The bed on the couch was his. As they left the room, Cultus pulled the blanket over himself, still dressed, the way Dan slept when he stayed with them.

The rest of the week went easier for Angie. The visit had

been a success, just sitting like that and watching TV, and although they hadn't talked about what they were going to do when they went to court, Angie felt more secure about it. Maybe more secure than if they *had* talked about it, since they would have argued. They didn't go back any night that week; it didn't seem necessary.

The girls went to school like always, with or without Cultus. On Saturday Katla did the laundry while the girls took long, steamy showers. And Sunday was spent at the Longhouse. It wasn't until Sunday night that the anxiety of appearing in court the next day returned to Angie.

She tried not to think about it, but she was nagged by a vague feeling of unrest that made her irritable. She argued with Carysa while they were folding the wing dresses to put them away; then again when Carysa was playing with the fire in the stove instead of just putting the wood into it; and finally Angie ended by socking her when she wouldn't lie still in bed.

Angie was so preoccupied with what lay ahead of them that she washed when Katla told her to instead of sneaking out of it. That woke her up, certainly, but she was so out of sorts that being awake only made her more miserable.

Even Dan was melancholy and touchy. Soon after he came to pick them up, he and Katla got into an argument about what time they were supposed to be in Red Salmon. The result was that Katla and Dan didn't speak to each other all the way to town and they arrived forty-five minutes early. It was a little weird, Angie thought to herself, that on the day they might have to prove that they should stay together as a family, no one was talking to anyone else.

"See, I told you so," Dan said spitefully when the policeman at the desk told them they could go on in, but they would have a long time to wait. At least Dan and Katla agreed that they would rather wait in the courtroom than down the street at Stacey's.

Without knowing it, Angie had been expecting something. Now, as she sat in the stuffy little room, empty except for the five of them, she realized that she had had an altogether different idea of what it would be like. What she saw was a room the size of a classroom, divided in half right down the middle by a plywood separator about waist high. The side they sat on had about thirty folding chairs in three uneven rows. That was all.

The other side of the room was more interesting. There was a place Angie recognized as the judge's. She remembered it was called a bench, although it didn't look like one. It was just a big plywood box, big enough to sit behind, but it looked small enough to be moved around, too.

Someone had lined up a row of chairs just over the divider, facing the bench, and one more chair stood beside it. This was where she expected Cultus would have to sit. There would be a lawyer for him and one against him, and they would question him until he cracked. Angie wondered where the jury would sit. She just didn't see how everybody was going to fit into this small room.

She was uncomfortable. It was warm in the room and her nerves only made her more sweaty. She didn't want to take her coat off because she was sure she would have big wet marks under her arms, so she sweltered all the more.

To her relief, no one spoke for some time. Then Carysa cupped her hand over Angie's ear to say something she couldn't understand. Angie just shook her head, annoyed that Carysa was embarrassing her. Carysa got up to tell Katla.

Once Angie had been carrying two Cokes to the pickup at the drive-in when Cultus had honked the horn. She had jumped so far that she dropped both Cokes onto her jeans. That's how she felt when Katla spoke to her now.

"Angie, take your little sister to the bathroom," she boomed. Then, "Why is everybody whispering?" she whispered. Angie took Carysa by the hand and found a lavatory.

When she came back she was relieved to see Jobie talking with Dan and Katla. "No, there won't be a lawyer here today," he explained. "Since Cultus plans to say he did take the pickup, he probably won't need one. It's only when you say you didn't do something that you need a lawyer—to defend you from the one who says you did do it. This won't be all that complicated. I talked with Cultus this morning, and I think everything will go all right for him today."

No lawyers? Angie was bewildered, but at least the room was friendlier with Jobie there. His voice sounded natural, not too loud and not whispering, as he explained to a dumbfounded Dan that lawyers were usually appointed when people decided they wanted a trial. This wasn't a trial.

The room had nearly filled—at least their half—when Jobie went out to bring in Cultus. He came back with him and three others, all older than Cultus but not much older. They sat on the chairs just over the divider.

Cultus looked excited and nervous. He turned around once, then turned back to face the bench almost at once. Angie wasn't sure whether they could talk to him, and was afraid someone might try only to be told to stop. Nobody did. The room was tense, hot, quiet.

Somebody said, "Everybody please stand." The voice was full of authority and Angie stood, feeling jerked up like a jack-in-the-box whose handle had been turned. The judge walked in with a flurry of robes. Angie, looking at him from the back, thought he must be an Indian. He had long hair, long enough for braids, but loose and not quite black, like a person of mixed blood.

When the judge turned to face the room from behind the plywood platform, Angie was shocked to see it was a white woman. She turned to exchange a look of disapproval with Katla, but her grandmother had a searching, woebegone look

158

that took in the entire room. Their eyes didn't meet.

"You may be seated," the voice said again. Angie turned to identify the voice; it came from the policeman who had told them they could wait in the courtroom. He went to the other side of the separator and stood leaning on the wall with his arms crossed.

Angie started when the woman hit a small hammer on something. She called the court to order; that, at least, was something she recognized from television. The rest of it was sometimes such a strange process that she didn't understand it, and sometimes so simple that she lost interest. Either way, she was disappointed.

Then Cultus was called and he stood up. He was told to state his name and address. Everyone else had been asked to do the same thing, but it seemed silly when it was his turn; everybody knew who he was, so why did he have to tell them again?

He looked at his feet and spoke so softly that he was asked to repeat it. Instead of making him speak up, however, it only made him more self-conscious, and the second time it was even harder to hear him.

The judge looked cross. "Bailiff," she said, and Jobie stood. "Will you instruct this young man to speak up?" Cultus looked scared, but Jobie merely had to nod his head and Cultus did as he was told.

"My name is Cultus Wolfe. I live with my Katla—that is,

my mother's mother—at her cabin on the Badger Creek Road."

"Thank you, Cultus," she said sharply. "What are the charges against him, Bailiff?" Jobie told her that Cultus was accused of stealing a pickup, and gave her the details including the license number and the name of the owner. He said that the man who owned the pickup wasn't in the courtroom because he had to work.

"Thank you," she replied curtly. With her eyes cutting into him, as if she could tell what he was thinking no matter what he said, she asked Cultus, "And what do you have to say for yourself, young man?"

Cultus's head hung, but he spoke up. "I done it, ma'am, Your Honor, just like he said."

"I *did* it, not I *done* it," she corrected him. Then she let the room fill with a tense silence, punishingly long, but during that time her face changed. She softened. Angie wondered if the woman could be trusted. She seemed downright sneaky, as if she could say one thing and mean another.

"Do you care to give the court an explanation? It might help us in our decision." She looked like she wanted Cultus to trust her now, but he didn't look up. Angie was sure he'd begun to cry, but she had no way of knowing from behind.

"Is your grandmother here—what was it you called her—Katla? Is she here today?" Cultus nodded yes, but didn't say anything. "In order to gain more of an insight into your case, I'd like the chance to talk with your family privately. Who is the grandmother?" she said, looking inquiringly to Angie's side of the room. Katla made a shy movement with her hand, the way kids did at school when the teacher asked a question they couldn't answer. She raised her hand like that, just enough to be recognized but not enough to be called on.

"Can you meet with me in my chambers about fifteen minutes after this court?" It wasn't a real question. It was an order. Katla probably didn't know what "chambers" meant, but she nodded, eyes full of worry. Angie thought: So this is how they're going to do it. Katla will be just as shy as Cultus, and this white woman's going to think that because Katla maybe can't talk like her that she's stupid. Then they'll take us away from her.

"Court is adjourned," the woman said, and tapped her little hammer again.

"Would you like to stay and talk with your family until she's ready to see you?" Jobie asked. Cultus stayed, and Jobie led the other three defendants out of the room.

Katla was so quiet that Angie was afraid to ask her what she was thinking. Her eyes were slits, like she had a headache. Angie didn't know whether having to see the judge in her chambers was a good turn for them or a bad one; she thought bad, but she wanted to know what the rest of them thought about it. She didn't have to ask Dan.

161

"Well, she don't seem exactly friendly, isn't it?" he said when they were alone in the room again.

Angie looked Cultus full in the face for the first time that day, and was surprised to see that he hadn't been crying.

"I wonder what she would have done if I hadn't answered her?" he muttered.

"I don't think you'd have gotten away with it," Jobie said, coming back into the room. "She's a pretty tough old gal, Judge Edwards. I guess she has to be. It isn't exactly easy being a judge. But she's fair, too."

When Jobie told them it was time they went to the judge's office—he didn't say "chambers"—Angie pictured that stern woman embarrassing them all with her questions and she didn't want to go. "Can I stay in here?" she begged. "I won't go anywhere. I promise. I could just wait for you here, Katla."

It was Jobie who answered her. "I'm sure Judge Edwards would be sorry not to have you there. You might be able to tell her something that would help."

So Angie followed them out of the courtroom and down the hall, but with her heels dragging and her hands in her pockets. Jobie held a door open for them and they filed in. Just before Angie went through the door, he jabbed her in the ribs and whispered, "Come on, don't be such a chicken!"

She walked into the room with a secret smile as Jobie closed the door behind himself.

13

J udge Edwards offered coffee to the adults, pointing to a pot on a small table beside her desk, but she didn't take any herself. Jobie was the only one who did. He was just neat, Angie thought, the way he wasn't scared of anything. But, then, they weren't trying to take him away from his Katla, either.

"Now then," she began, "I hope this is a little better. Cultus, what I want to find out is why you are getting into trouble, because I think that if we can find out why you're doing these things we can put a stop to them. But first, I'd like to get acquainted here," she said, looking at each of them boldly.

She started with Dan. He explained that he was Cultus's uncle, his mother's brother. He said that he was also Carysa's and Angie's uncle, but their mother had been his other sister. She thanked him and asked which one was Angie. Carysa pointed to her and Angie shriveled as if the judge's eyes were cold water.

"That's her. That's Angie," Carysa said. "She just eggs nore everybody today. And I'm Carysa."

The judge smiled and said, "You mean *ignores*. She ignores me, not eggs nore."

"That's not what *I* say," Carysa replied arrogantly.

"And this young lady, who are you?" she asked Marta. Carysa answered, "Oh, that's Marta," and the judge had to ask her to let the young lady speak for herself. Angie made a face. The way she corrected everybody, and all this "young man" and "young lady" stuff made her sound like a teacher about to scold.

Marta explained that she was Cultus's sister, and then shut up so abruptly that it was noticeable. The judge didn't seem to let Marta's rudeness bother her, however. "I guess that's everyone," she said, "except Officer Sohappy, and I'm sure you all know him."

Turning to Cultus, she said, "Now, I want to hear all about this, clear from the beginning. Cultus, what were you doing downtown in the first place? Or, I guess there's something here about a fight with the bus driver." She opened a folder and laid it flat on the desk in front of her before continuing. "Perhaps you should start with that."

"Your Honor?" It was Dan, his voice deeper than usual. Everyone looked at him with surprise, and as he talked, his voice got squeaky. "I think Cultus might leave part of it out.

164

I mean about that Tewet girl that he pushed. She pushed his grandma a week ago and broke her arm. That's why she's got it in a cast," he said.

"I wondered how that happened. I didn't know anything about that." She asked Katla a few questions about her arm, and made her tell the whole story while she wrote some of it down in the folder.

"Lois knew I wouldn't really hurt her," Cultus muttered when Katla was finished.

"Hmm," the judge said, as if that were interesting. Angie decided that she hated this lady because there was no way of knowing what she was thinking.

"But you wanted the driver to think you were going to hurt her. I say that because I notice here that you were suspended from the bus just last week for something similar. Isn't that right?"

Cultus seemed to give up. He shrugged, looking at the floor, and said, "I guess so." If she knows all the answers, why does she ask, Angie wondered.

"You knew you weren't going to hurt Lois, but you made it look that way so you could provoke a fight with the driver," the lady went on. "Then when you ran away from the bus, you saw the pickup running in front of the post office and decided to take it. Were you thinking that a little more trouble wouldn't make any difference? Is that why you took it?"

Cultus looked at the rest of his family instead of answering. The look seemed to be saying, "How can I tell a white woman?"

"You don't understand," Cultus said. Everybody squirmed, but Judge Edwards was the only one who spoke.

"Maybe I do," she said. "I understand young people well enough to know that sometimes they don't have to know their reasons for getting into trouble. Sometimes they don't even have reasons. Is that how it is with you, Cultus? Are you just a troublemaker?"

Cultus didn't answer, but everybody else did. Angie had shouted, "That's not true," before she noticed that everyone was talking at once. Angie thought Judge Edwards should pound her little hammer on her desk until everyone was quiet, but she didn't seem to have it. And she proved she didn't really need it. After she had watched enough of this, looking calmly from face to face, all she did was stand up. The room grew quiet. Everybody looked as if they'd let out some secret. Judge Edwards sat down again and looked hard at all of them.

"Now I'd like to hear what this is all about. Who would like to start?" she asked.

"I'll tell you what it is, it's . . ." Dan started, but Katla cut him off.

"You shut up," she exclaimed. Then she repeated the order in Indian, this time apologetically. *"Paiknm,"* she said,

166

"listen to me," but she had hurt Dan's feelings all the same.

"Maybe I shouldn't talk," she told the judge. "Maybe I say things you don't like if I talk. Then you take my kids away from me. So I don't want to say them things."

"Oh good heavens, no!" the judge declared. "Who in the world ever told you that I would even consider taking these children away from you?" Katla didn't answer, but she looked accusingly at Dan. Angie looked at Dan a little unkindly herself. He had caused her a lot of worry for nothing.

"Why, if it weren't for the grandmothers I don't know who would raise all the children whose parents are gone for one reason or another. I imagine that more children here live with grandparents rather than their true parents. Certainly the Group Home couldn't raise them. No. I have no doubt that you have given Cultus and the girls a good home. Please don't even think I would consider changing that.

"And do tell me what you're thinking. I'm sure it will help us decide what we can do to help Cultus." As she talked, the woman had played nervously with her pencil, but Angie observed that by the time she finished talking her businesslike manner had returned. She refolded her hands in front of her and waited for Katla's reply.

Angie feared, in the long pause that followed, that Katla had forgotten what she had to say. She did that sometimes. But finally her grandmother began to speak.

"I'm only a old woman. I don't talk such good English,"

167

she started, and Angie recognized the familiar theme. Angie knew she was about to tell the judge how helpless she was, and how she couldn't read or write, and how nobody helped her at home. But then Katla surprised her.

"And so when my kids come home from school they tell me this and they tell me that and I don't understand a lot of the time. Maybe I don't listen so good. For a long time I look at Cultus and I think like you say. 'Yeah, Cultus, he's just a bad one,' I think. But listen.

"These kids, all my kids, like goin' to school but only so far. Dan here, he never liked it, but that was the boarding school. That was different. That was takin' kids away from their parents and their people and so nobody liked that boarding school. We was all glad we got rid of it.

"But it's different for these kids. My kids come home at night now. I raise 'em, not nobody else. And I don't raise 'em to be like no apple, all red on the outside and white in the middle.

"And so I raise my kids the way I think's right. Not with maybe a Powwow or a root feast once a year and drunk all the rest of the time like some. And I don't dress my kids Indian 'cause I think it's cute or eat Indian foods 'cause it's free. No! We live Indian 'cause that's what we are.

"And then I watch 'em go to school. They all like it when they go here on the reservation, up to sixth grade. All them other kids is Indian and the boys wear braids and they ain't ashamed.

"Then they gotta leave here and go to them junior high in Baker. And as soon as they do that it's like something goes *bump*"—and Katla lurched in her chair to show her how—"and then they stop liking school. And that ain't all.

"It's worse for boys, but even Angie there is different now that she goes to them Baker school. She's a different person. Now she don't talk Indian, she makes fun of it. Even at home she won't talk it. And she won't dress Indian or nothin', only at Powwow and Sunday, and I don't like it. This year, she wants a buffalo dress, only she don't want to learn nothin' so she can make it herself. They don't listen at home, and they push me around or swear at me, them kids. The *old* people, their own people, they're ashamed of us."

Angie listened to this and burned with shame. How much it had mattered to Katla! She vowed to herself that she would earn her dress next year.

"Now I go to that school and I see. There ain't nobody tells them to cut their hair that I can see. Nobody makes fun of them. It's all inside our own kids. It's like they go there and they drink poison. Or maybe it's like what Dan here all the time saying. Maybe it's what they make 'em learn, only I don't think so. Let me tell you how I mean.

"Angie, she's learnin' Health. I go there and see and

169

that's a nice lady. What she teachin' Angie she needs to know. But I keep Angie out to help with the Powwow. And the teacher don't think that's important.

"Powwow, that ain't important? Someday Marta, maybe Angie, gotta take my place in that Longhouse. *That* gonna be their test and I gotta teach 'em for it. Now listen. What I wanta know is this. Why ever since the beginning of the whites teachin' our kids they think Indians ain't got nothin' to teach their own children? I know something, by damn! And so do these kids! But maybe it ain't important, what we know? We believe that, and then pretty soon no more Indians. Only apples." And Katla stopped, looking out the window beside her as if, having said everything she had to say, she was now ready to leave.

Angie was mistaken, though. Katla wasn't finished. She had paused to think and when she spoke this time it was slowly, unsurely. She looked at Cultus the whole time as if trying to figure out from him what she should say.

"Cultus, he's one of them apples, too. I look at him and I see how he's lost inside, and that's like Angie. He stopped talkin' Indian and dressin' Indian and he won't dance. He's lost and he don't know what to do, he's just mad. So he tries to run away. He stole a truck."

Katla paused, staring right into Cultus. When she spoke again she was shouting so loudly that Angie jumped and everyone else looked startled, too.

170

"And I tell you something right now, Cultus Wolfe. It's like I'm seeing you for the first time and maybe I'm wrong. Maybe you're a bad, bad boy like they say, but I'm proud of you 'cause you're strong and 'cause you struggle so hard."

The words "so hard" seemed to hang in the silence that followed. Judge Edwards looked stunned. Angie tried to get Cultus's eyes, but he was staring at Katla. She wanted to say something, "I'll try," or "I understand," but the silence was like a cloud she couldn't get through. It made her furious, and she slammed her hand down on her thigh so hard that it brought tears to her eyes. And the slap made everyone look at her. She was embarrassed.

"I'm glad you were able to tell me this," Judge Edwards said sincerely. "I think it would do some good if you could talk about it again, to tell the right people. You see, I'm involved with the schools, too. The tribe is meeting with the school board in the Tribal Council chambers next month, and I would like to have you come and tell those people what you've just told me." There was an awkward pause in which Katla didn't answer. She had said what she was going to say, and now it was time to think again.

"Judge Edwards?" It was Jobie. Angie had forgotten he was in the room. He waited for the judge to acknowledge him before he went on.

"Yes, Officer Sohappy," she responded.

"Your Honor, I've taken a personal interest in Cultus, and

I would like to suggest that, if you're considering a period of probation for him, I'd like to serve the court as his probation officer."

"Certainly. I was hoping you'd agree to do it. Now, Cultus," she said, although she was obviously talking to Katla, "I've decided to release you in a week's time from the Group Home to serve a period of two years under probation. During that time you will report to Officer Sohappy regularly and you will remain in the custody of your grandmother."

Angie became bored with the rest. She wondered if anybody listened as Judge Edwards explained what Cultus was expected to do. She ended with a stern warning that if he got into trouble while he was on probation it would be "very serious indeed." Angie was squirmy and anxious to stretch.

She sensed that the meeting was over before the judge said, "That will be all for today." At the door she heard Judge Edwards add, "Oh, and Mrs. Wallutala, I hope you'll consider what I said and come to the meeting next month. I'll be in touch with you about it."

~~~~~

14

"I don't go to no meetings," Katla muttered as they were leaving. The others seemed too tired to talk. Angie felt like a nap and couldn't wait to lie down in the back of the pickup. She knew that the things Katla had said to Judge Edwards were things for her to think about over and over again, but not now. Now was too soon, and the strain of the afternoon left her wanting to forget about it for a while.

They all walked out together. Jobie was going to take Cultus back to the Group Home, but in the parking lot he offered to buy everyone ice cream cones. They walked in a group to Stacey's.

"You said some fine things in there," Jobie said to Katla as he held the door open for her. He spoke to her in Indian language.

"I felt like she was making fun of me with all those questions," Katla grumped back. "I never should have said anything." She was really cranky and Jobie let it go for a few minutes. They got their ice cream cones and Jobie paid for them.

"I hope you'll change your mind and go to the meeting next month," he said.

"I don't go to no meetings," Katla spat out in English. "I made a big enough fool out of myself. I couldn't talk like that in front of the council and them white people from Baker. No!"

"Well, you have a while to think about it." And Jobie let the matter drop. They finished their ice cream cones and began walking back to the police station. Katla and Dan were ahead of Jobie and the children. Jobie seemed to be hanging back when he began talking to them.

"You three girls had better help her change her mind about that meeting. Nobody ever has the nerve to speak up at the right time. It's one thing to bellyache about something at home or in the Longhouse among your friends and another to speak up in front of a group of strangers. Your Katla has real courage, and maybe if you can convince her how important it is to go to that meeting, maybe then those people from Baker can learn something about us. I think they want to learn. They just need a good teacher, like your grandma. You better tell her that, Angie.

"Better wait a couple of days, though," he added with a smile and a look in Katla's direction.

———

Cultus hadn't ridden the bus since the day he stole the pickup, so Angie was surprised, a week after his day in court, to see him climb on. This was the day he was coming home, but she had expected Jobie to drive him to the cabin. He sat in the seat behind the driver. Angie wondered if that would be permanent.

Carysa ran on ahead to tell Katla that Cultus was home when they got off at their stop. Angie, Marta, and Cultus were shy with each other. They were halfway up the road before Angie asked, "How was it, Cultus?" What she meant was, What are you thinking? He seemed to know.

"We talked about stuff," he said. "You know. Jobie and me. He said that Indians used to steal horses from one another. It was kind of like a war game, and he told me that taking that pickup might have been like that. It's funny to hear a cop tell you that you done the right thing to steal."

"He said that?" Marta asked.

"Well, sort of. He said that before things was to get better for us more people had to go through what I did. He said it's like the old days, in a way. Like when the Whipman would send boys off alone without food. That's how the old ones found their medicine, and that's what was good about that mess with the truck. When the Whipman sent boys off alone, only the strong ones made it back. Jobie said he thought I was a strong one."

"So?"

"So I'm going to show them white people who's strong. I'm going to show them I ain't afraid to be Indian. That I

175

ain't stupid just 'cause I believe in the Indian ways."

Angie wanted to ask, Do you believe in them? She couldn't, of course. But she wanted to know what this belief of Cultus's amounted to. She was too impatient to wait and see.

"What are you going to do?" she asked, hoping again that Cultus would answer the question she couldn't ask.

"Well, Jobie says that if I can stay out of trouble he'll help me become a hunter. If Katla will help too, that is."

So he really was going to try, Angie thought. Becoming a hunter was more than killing a deer. The hunt dance and the Longhouse ceremony of the first kill was the traditional way an Indian boy became ready for manhood. Katla would have to prepare a feast and have a give-away. It would be expensive and hard work for her.

They were on the porch now, and Cultus smiled secretly to them before they went into the cabin.

Katla acted as if he'd never been away. "Cultus, before you do anything you go out back and take care of the smokehouse," she said. "I ain't goin' to have no lazy boy . . ."

"All right, all right," Cultus said, laughing. They were glad he was home.

~~~~~

Angie wasn't as tired the next morning as she expected to be. She felt fine, almost in spite of herself.

She went out to wash, but stopped at the porch when she heard a lark. She couldn't tell where it was. At first it sounded as if it were singing from near the smokehouse, behind her, then from the cheat grass growing in clumps by the road, then again from the smokehouse. Its song was insistent, as if telling her the same thing over and over again. Then Carysa came out.

"What's it saying?" Angie asked her.

"What's *what* saying?"

"The lark, silly. Listen to it."

"It's saying you better wash, Angie, 'cause I'll tell."

"No, it ain't. Why are you always such a little twerp?" But Angie walked to the pump with her little sister. "You know, it's supposed to tell you your future," she explained.

The lark sang again, and this time instead of trying to figure out where it was, Angie listened to the words.

"*Niih maitski!* That's what it says. Good morning!"

"Aw . . ." Carysa said.

"It does too. Listen!" But Carysa wasn't listening. She was daring Angie to start a water fight. Angie felt good, so she indulged her little sister. She made a face and stuck out her tongue—and got splashed. They went back into the cabin giggling, with water dripping from their braids.

The Whipman is Watching

T. A. Dyer

They all lived with their grandmother, but they were all so different.

Marta She accepted the Indian ways, even seemed proud of them. She almost always won the prize each year for the best girl dancer at the Powwow.

Angie She hated being different from the white kids they saw each day at the high school outside the reservation. But still, it was easier just to get along and not think too deeply about things.

Cultus He never could get along. He was always getting into trouble. On the bus, at school, at home. He even hit Katla once, their own grandmother.

And what scared Angie was that she half understood why he was so angry all the time. Because for her too, sometimes being a kid was like having a disease that was going to kill you. Adults were no help. At school, Mr. McGilvra, the principal, treated them with so much understanding you could choke on it, and at home Katla could only glare at Cultus and the others and go into her familiar diatribe about the good old days when the Indian Whipman had control over all the kids.

In this hard-hitting, gritty account of life for present-day Indian youth, T. A. Dyer, who has spent many years on a reservation in the Northwest, explores without sentimentality the twin problems of being Indian and being young in a world that sometimes seems to have room for neither.